THE NECKLACE AND OTHER SHORT STORIES

DOVER THRIFT EDITIONS

Guy de Maupassant

DOVER PUBLICATIONS, INC.
MINEOLA, NEW YORK

DOVER THRIFT EDITIONS

Editor: Stanley Appelbaum

Bibliographical Note

This Dover edition, first published in 1992, is an unabridged republication of nine stories. "Ball-of-Fat," "The Necklace," "A Piece of String," "Mme. Tellier's Establishment," "Mademoiselle Fifi," "Miss Harriet" and "A Way to Wealth" are reprinted from *The Works of Guy de Maupassant: Short Stories*, Black's Readers Service, Roslyn, N.Y., n.d. ("The Necklace" appears there as "The Diamond Necklace"; "Mme. Tellier's Establishment," as "Mme. Tellier's Excursion.") "My Uncle Jules" and "The Horla" are reprinted from standard translated editions.

Library of Congress Cataloging-in-Publication Data

Maupassant, Guy de, 1850–1893.
[Short stories. English. Selections]
The necklace and other short stories / Guy de Maupassant.
p.   cm. — (Dover thrift editions)
"An Unabridged republication of nine stories"—CIP ser. t.p.
ISBN-13: 978-0-486-27064-7 (pbk.)
ISBN-10: 0-486-27064-5 (pbk.)
1. Maupassant, Guy de, 1850–1893—Translations into English.
I. Title.   II. Series.
PQ2349.A4E5   1992
843'.8—dc20   91-28194
                                                  CIP

Manufactured in the United States by LSC Communications
27064513   2017
www.doverpublications.com

Note

THE FRENCH NOVELIST and short-story writer Guy de Maupassant (1850–1893) has entertained generations of readers and has influenced generations of authors (Maugham and O. Henry come immediately to mind). The present selection of nine famous stories represent such important traits and components of Maupassant's work as his ironic twists of plot, his fascination with prostitutes, his intimate knowledge of the landscape and inhabitants of Normandy, his obsession with the Franco-Prussian War (in which he served) and his interest in abnormal psychology (heightened by his own syphilitic neurasthenia).

Contents

The dates in brackets are those of the first (original French) publications of the stories in collected volumes (most appeared earlier in magazines).

Ball-of-Fat (Boule de Suif)

FOR MANY DAYS now the fag-end of the army had been straggling through the town. They were not troops, but a disbanded horde. The beards of the men were long and filthy, their uniforms in tatters, and they advanced at an easy pace without flag or regiment. All seemed worn-out and back-broken, incapable of a thought or a resolution, marching by habit solely, and falling from fatigue as soon as they stopped. In short, they were a mobilized, pacific people, bending under the weight of the gun; some little squads on the alert, easy to take alarm and prompt in enthusiasm, ready to attack or to flee; and in the midst of them, some red breeches, the remains of a division broken up in a great battle; some somber artillery men in line with these varied kinds of foot soldiers; and, sometimes the brilliant helmet of a dragoon on foot who followed with difficulty the shortest march of the lines.

Some legions of free-shooters, under the heroic names of "Avengers of the Defeat," "Citizens of the Tomb," "Partakers of Death," passed in their turn with the air of bandits.

Their leaders were former cloth or grain merchants, ex-merchants in tallow or soap, warriors of circumstance, elected officers on account of their escutcheons and the length of their mustaches, covered with arms and with braid, speaking in constrained voices, discussing plans of campaign, and pretending to carry agonized France alone on their swaggering shoulders, but sometimes fearing their own soldiers, prison-birds, that were often brave at first and later proved to be plunderers and debauchees.

It was said that the Prussians were going to enter Rouen.

The National Guard who for two months had been carefully reconnoitering in the neighboring woods, shooting sometimes their own sentinels, and ready for a combat whenever a little wolf stirred in the thicket, had now returned to their firesides. Their arms, their uniforms, all the murderous

1

accoutrements with which they had lately struck fear into the national heart for three leagues in every direction, had suddenly disappeared.

The last French soldiers finally came across the Seine to reach the Audemer bridge through Saint-Sever and Bourg-Achard; and, marching behind, on foot, between two officers of ordnance, the General, in despair, unable to do anything with these incongruous tatters, himself lost in the breaking-up of a people accustomed to conquer, and disastrously beaten, in spite of his legendary bravery.

A profound calm, a frightful, silent expectancy had spread over the city. Many of the heavy citizens, emasculated by commerce, anxiously awaited the conquerors, trembling lest their roasting spits or kitchen knives be considered arms.

All life seemed stopped; shops were closed, the streets dumb. Sometimes an inhabitant, intimidated by this silence, moved rapidly along next the walls. The agony of waiting made them wish the enemy would come.

In the afternoon of the day which followed the departure of the French troops, some uhlans, coming from one knows not where, crossed the town with celerity. Then, a little later, a black mass descended the side of St. Catharine, while two other invading bands appeared by the way of Darnetal and Boisguillaume. The advance guard of the three bodies joined one another at the same moment in Hôtel de Ville square and, by all the neighboring streets, the German army continued to arrive, spreading out its battalions, making the pavement resound under their hard, rhythmic step.

Some orders of the commander, in a foreign, guttural voice, reached the houses which seemed dead and deserted, while behind closed shutters, eyes were watching these victorious men, masters of the city, of fortunes, of lives, through the "rights of war." The inhabitants, shut up in their rooms, were visited with the kind of excitement that a cataclysm, or some fatal upheaval of the earth, brings to us, against which all force is useless. For the same sensation is produced each time that the established order of things is overturned, when security no longer exists, and all that protect the laws of man and of nature find themselves at the mercy of unreasoning, ferocious brutality. The trembling of the earth crushing the houses and burying an entire people; a river overflowing its banks and carrying in its course the drowned peasants, carcasses of beeves, and girders snatched from roofs, or a glorious army massacring those trying to defend themselves, leading others prisoners, pillaging in the name of the sword and thanking God to the sound of the cannon, all are alike frightful scourges which disconnect all belief in eternal justice, all the confidence that we have in the protection of Heaven and the reason of man.

Some detachments rapped at each door, then disappeared into the houses. It was occupation after invasion. Then the duty commences for the conquered to show themselves gracious toward the conquerors.

After some time, as soon as the first terror disappears, a new calm is established. In many families, the Prussian officer eats at the table. He is sometimes well bred and, through politeness, pities France, and speaks of his repugnance in taking part in this affair. One is grateful to him for this sentiment; then, one may be, some day or other, in need of his protection. By treating him well, one has, perhaps, a less number of men to feed. And why should we wound anyone on whom we are entirely dependent? To act thus would be less bravery than temerity. And temerity is no longer a fault of the commoner of Rouen, as it was at the time of the heroic defense, when their city became famous. Finally, each told himself that the highest judgment of French urbanity required that they be allowed to be polite to the strange soldier in the house, provided they did not show themselves familiar with him in public. Outside they would not make themselves known to each other, but at home they could chat freely, and the German might remain longer each evening warming his feet at their hearthstones.

The town even took on, little by little, its ordinary aspect. The French scarcely went out, but the Prussian soldiers grumbled in the streets. In short, the officers of the Blue Hussars, who dragged with arrogance their great weapons of death up and down the pavement, seemed to have no more grievous scorn for the simple citizens than the officers or the sportsmen who, the year before, drank in the same *cafés*.

There was, nevertheless, something in the air, something subtle and unknown, a strange, intolerable atmosphere like a penetrating odor, the odor of invasion. It filled the dwellings and the public places, changed the taste of the food, gave the impression of being on a journey, far away, among barbarous and dangerous tribes.

The conquerors exacted money, much money. The inhabitants always paid and they were rich enough to do it. But the richer a trading Norman becomes the more he suffers at every outlay, at each part of his fortune that he sees pass from his hands into those of another.

Therefore, two or three leagues below the town, following the course of the river toward Croisset, Dieppedalle, or Biessart mariners and fishermen often picked up the swollen corpse of a German in uniform from the bottom of the river, killed by the blow of a knife, the head crushed with a stone, or perhaps thrown into the water by a push from the high bridge. The slime of the river bed buried these obscure vengeances, savage, but legitimate, unknown heroisms, mute attacks more perilous than the battles of broad day, and without the echoing sound of glory.

For hatred of the foreigner always arouses some intrepid ones, who are ready to die for an idea.

Finally, as soon as the invaders had brought the town quite under subjection with their inflexible discipline, without having been guilty of any of the horrors for which they were famous along their triumphal line of march, people began to take courage, and the need of trade put new heart into the commerce of the country. Some had large interests at Havre, which the French army occupied, and they wished to try and reach this port by going to Dieppe by land and there embarking.

They used their influence with the German soldiers with whom they had an acquaintance, and finally, an authorization of departure was obtained from the General-in-chief.

Then, a large diligence, with four horses, having been engaged for this journey, and ten persons having engaged seats in it, it was resolved to set out on Tuesday morning before daylight, in order to escape observation.

For some time before, the frost had been hardening the earth and on Monday, toward three o'clock, great black clouds coming from the north brought the snow which fell without interruption during the evening and all night.

At half past four in the morning, the travelers met in the courtyard of Hôtel Normandie, where they were to take the carriage.

They were still full of sleep, and shivering with cold under their wraps. They could only see each other dimly in the obscure light, and the accumulation of heavy winter garments made them all resemble fat curates in long cassocks. Only two of the men were acquainted; a third accosted them and they chatted: "I'm going to take my wife," said one. "I too," said another. "And I," said the third. The first added: "We shall not return to Rouen, and if the Prussians approach Havre, we shall go over to England." All had the same projects, being of the same mind.

As yet the horses were not harnessed. A little lantern, carried by a stable hand, went out one door from time to time, to immediately appear at another. The feet of the horses striking the floor could be heard, although deadened by the straw and litter, and the voice of a man talking to the beasts, sometimes swearing, came from the end of the building. A light tinkling of bells announced that they were taking down the harness; this murmur soon became a clear and continuous rhythm by the movement of the animal, stopping sometimes, then breaking into a brusque shake which was accompanied by the dull stamp of a hoof upon the hard earth.

The door suddenly closed. All noise ceased. The frozen citizens were silent; they remained immovable and stiff.

A curtain of uninterrupted white flakes constantly sparkled in its descent to the ground. It effaced forms, and powdered everything with a downy moss. And nothing could be heard in the great silence. The town was calm, and buried under the wintry frost, as this fall of snow, unnamable and floating, a sensation rather than a sound (trembling atoms which only seem to fill all space), came to cover the earth.

The man reappeared with his lantern, pulling at the end of a rope a sad horse which would not come willingly. He placed him against the pole, fastened the traces, walked about a long time adjusting the harness, for he had the use of but one hand, the other carrying the lantern. As he went for the second horse, he noticed the travelers, motionless, already white with snow, and said to them: "Why not get into the carriage? You will be under cover, at least."

They had evidently not thought of it, and they hastened to do so. The three men installed their wives at the back and then followed them. Then the other forms, undecided and veiled, took in their turn the last places without exchanging a word.

The floor was covered with straw, in which the feet ensconced themselves. The ladies at the back having brought little copper foot stoves, with a carbon fire, lighted them and, for some time, in low voices, enumerated the advantages of the appliances, repeating things that they had known for a long time.

Finally, the carriage was harnessed with six horses instead of four, because the traveling was very bad, and a voice called out:

"Is everybody aboard?"

And a voice within answered: "Yes."

They were off. The carriage moved slowly, slowly for a little way. The wheels were imbedded in the snow; the whole body groaned with heavy cracking sounds; the horses glistened, puffed, and smoked; and the great whip of the driver snapped without ceasing, hovering about on all sides, knotting and unrolling itself like a thin serpent, lashing brusquely some horse on the rebound, which then put forth its most violent effort.

Now the day was imperceptibly dawning. The light flakes, which one of the travelers, a Rouenese by birth, said looked like a shower of cotton, no longer fell. A faint light filtered through the great dull clouds, which rendered more brilliant the white of the fields, where appeared a line of great trees clothed in whiteness, or a chimney with a cap of snow.

In the carriage, each looked at the others curiously, in the sad light of this dawn.

At the back, in the best places, Mr. Loiseau, wholesale merchant of wine, of Grand-Pont street, and Mrs. Loiseau were sleeping opposite each other. Loiseau had bought out his former patron who failed in business, and made his fortune. He sold bad wine at a good price to small retailers in the country, and passed among his friends and acquaintances as a knavish wag, a true Norman full of deceit and joviality.

His reputation as a sharper was so well established that one evening at the residence of the prefect, Mr. Tournel, author of some fables and songs, of keen, satirical mind, a local celebrity, having proposed to some ladies, who seemed to be getting a little sleepy, that they make up a game of "Loiseau tricks," the joke traversed the rooms of the prefect, reached those of the town, and then, in the months to come, made many a face in the province expand with laughter.

Loiseau was especially known for his love of farce of every kind, for his jokes, good and bad; and no one could ever talk with him without thinking: "He is invaluable, this Loiseau." Of tall figure, his balloon-shaped front was surmounted by a ruddy face surrounded by gray whiskers.

His wife, large, strong, and resolute, with a quick, decisive manner, was the order and arithmetic of this house of commerce, while he was the life of it through his joyous activity.

Beside them, Mr. Carré-Lamadon held himself with great dignity, as if belonging to a superior caste; a considerable man, in cottons, proprietor of three mills, officer of the Legion of Honor, and member of the General Council. He had remained, during the Empire, chief of the friendly opposition, famous for making the Emperor pay more dear for rallying to the cause than if he had combated it with blunted arms, according to his own story. Madame Carré-Lamadon, much younger than her husband, was the consolation of officers of good family sent to Rouen in garrison. She sat opposite her husband, very dainty, petite, and pretty, wrapped closely in furs and looking with sad eyes at the interior of the carriage.

Her neighbors, the Count and Countess Hubert de Breville, bore the name of one of the most ancient and noble families of Normandy. The Count, an old gentleman of good figure, accentuated, by the artifices of his toilette, his resemblance to King Henry IV., who, following a glorious legend of the family, had impregnated one of the De Breville ladies, whose husband, for this reason, was made a count and governor of the province.

A colleague of Mr. Carré-Lamadon in the General Council, Count Hubert represented the Orléans party in the Department.

The story of his marriage with the daughter of a little captain of a privateer had always remained a mystery. But as the Countess had a grand air, received better than anyone, and passed for having been loved by the son of Louis Philippe, all the nobility did her honor, and her salon remained the first in the country, the only one which preserved the old gallantry, and to which the *entrée* was difficult. The fortune of the Brevilles amounted, it was said, to five hundred thousand francs in income, all in good securities.

These six persons formed the foundation of the carriage company, the society side, serene and strong, honest, established people, who had both religion and principles.

By a strange chance, all the women were upon the same seat; and the

Countess had for neighbors two sisters who picked at long strings of beads and muttered some *Paters* and *Aves*. One was old and as pitted with smallpox as if she had received a broadside of grapeshot full in the face. The other, very sad, had a pretty face and a disease of the lungs, which, added to their devoted faith, illumined them and made them appear like martyrs.

Opposite these two devotees were a man and a woman who attracted the notice of all. The man, well known, was Cornudet the democrat, the terror of respectable people. For twenty years he had soaked his great red beard in the *bocks* of all the democratic *cafés*. He had consumed with his friends and *confrères* a rather pretty fortune left him by his father, an old confectioner, and he awaited the establishing of the Republic with impatience, that he might have the position he merited by his great expenditures. On the fourth of September, by some joke perhaps, he believed himself elected prefect, but when he went to assume the duties, the clerks of the office were masters of the place and refused to recognize him, obliging him to retreat. Rather a good bachelor, on the whole, inoffensive and serviceable, he had busied himself, with incomparable ardor, in organizing the defense against the Prussians. He had dug holes in all the plains, cut down young trees from the neighboring forests, sown snares over all routes and, at the approach of the enemy, took himself quickly back to the town. He now thought he could be of more use in Havre where more entrenchments would be necessary.

The woman, one of those called a coquette, was celebrated for her *embonpoint*, which had given her the nickname of "Ball-of-Fat." Small, round, and fat as lard, with puffy fingers choked at the phalanges, like chaplets of short sausages; with a stretched and shining skin, an enormous bosom which shook under her dress, she was, nevertheless, pleasing and sought after, on account of a certain freshness and breeziness of disposition. Her face was a round apple, a peony bud ready to pop into bloom, and inside that opened two great black eyes, shaded with thick brows that cast a shadow within; and below, a charming mouth, humid for kissing, furnished with shining, microscopic baby teeth. She was, it was said, full of admirable qualities.

As soon as she was recognized, a whisper went around among the honest women, and the words "prostitute" and "public shame" were whispered so loud that she raised her head. Then she threw at her neighbors such a provoking, courageous look that a great silence reigned, and everybody looked down except Loiseau, who watched her with an exhilarated air.

And immediately conversation began among the three ladies, whom the presence of this girl had suddenly rendered friendly, almost intimate. It seemed to them they should bring their married dignity into union in opposition to that sold without shame; for legal love always takes on a tone of contempt for its free *confrère*.

The three men, also drawn together by an instinct of preservation at the sight of Cornudet, talked money with a certain high tone of disdain for the poor. Count Hubert talked of the havoc which the Prussians had caused, the losses which resulted from being robbed of cattle and from destroyed crops, with the assurance of a great lord, ten times millionaire, whom these ravages would scarcely cramp for a year. Mr. Carré-Lamadon, largely experienced in the cotton industry, had had need of sending six hundred thousand francs to England, as a trifle in reserve if it should be needed. As for Loiseau, he had arranged with the French administration to sell them all the wines that remained in his cellars, on account of which the State owed him a formidable sum, which he counted on collecting at Havre.

And all three threw toward each other swift and amicable glances.

Although in different conditions, they felt themselves to be brothers through money, that grand free-masonry of those who possess it, and make the gold rattle by putting their hands in their trousers' pockets.

The carriage went so slowly that at ten o'clock in the morning they had not gone four leagues. The men had got down three times to climb hills on foot. They began to be disturbed because they should be now taking breakfast at Tôtes and they despaired now of reaching there before night. Each one had begun to watch for an inn along the route, when the carriage foundered in a snowdrift, and it took two hours to extricate it.

Growing appetites troubled their minds; and no eating-house, no wine shop showed itself, the approach of the Prussians and the passage of the troops having frightened away all these industries.

The gentlemen ran to the farms along the way for provisions, but they did not even find bread, for the defiant peasant had concealed his stores for fear of being pillaged by the soldiers who, having nothing to put between their teeth, took by force whatever they discovered.

Toward one o'clock in the afternoon, Loiseau announced that there was a decided hollow in his stomach. Everybody suffered with him, and the violent need of eating, ever increasing, had killed conversation.

From time to time some one yawned; another immediately imitated him; and each, in his turn, in accordance with his character, his knowledge of life, and his social position, opened his mouth with carelessness or modesty, placing his hand quickly before the yawning hole from whence issued a vapor.

Ball-of-Fat, after many attempts, bent down as if seeking something under her skirts. She hesitated a second, looked at her neighbors, then sat up again tranquilly. The faces were pale and drawn. Loiseau affirmed that he would give a thousand francs for a small ham. His wife made a gesture, as if in protest; but she kept quiet. She was always troubled when anyone spoke of squandering money, and could not comprehend any pleasantry on the subject. "The fact is," said the Count, "I cannot understand why I did not think to bring some provisions with me." Each reproached himself in the same way.

However, Cornudet had a flask full of rum. He offered it; it was refused coldly. Loiseau alone accepted two swallows, and then passed back the flask saying, by way of thanks: "It is good all the same; it is warming and checks the appetite." The alcohol put him in good-humor and he proposed that they do as they did on the little ship in the song, eat the fattest of the passengers. This indirect allusion to Ball-of-Fat choked the well-bred people. They said nothing. Cornudet alone laughed. The two good sisters had ceased to mumble their rosaries and, with their hands enfolded in their great sleeves, held themselves immovable, obstinately lowering their eyes, without doubt offering to Heaven the suffering it had brought upon them.

Finally at three o'clock, when they found themselves in the midst of an interminable plain, without a single village in sight, Ball-of-Fat bending down quickly drew from under the seat a large basket covered with a white napkin.

At first she brought out a little china plate and a silver cup; then a large dish in which there were two whole chickens, cut up and imbedded in their own jelly. And one could still see in the basket other good things, some *pâtés*, fruits, and sweetmeats, provisions for three days if they should not see the kitchen of an inn. Four necks of bottles were seen among the packages of food. She took a wing of a chicken and began to eat it delicately, with one of those little biscuits called "Regence" in Normandy.

All looks were turned in her direction. Then the odor spread, enlarging the nostrils and making the mouth water, besides causing a painful contraction of the jaw behind the ears. The scorn of the women for this girl became ferocious, as if they had a desire to kill her and throw her out of the carriage into the snow, her, her silver cup, her basket, provisions and all.

But Loiseau with his eyes devoured the dish of chicken. He said: "Fortunately Madame had more precaution than we. There are some people who know how to think ahead always."

She turned toward him, saying: "If you would like some of it, sir? It is hard to go without breakfast so long."

He saluted her and replied: "Faith, I frankly cannot refuse; I can stand it no longer. Everything goes in time of war, does it not, Madame?" And then casting a comprehensive glance around, he added: "In moments like this, one can but be pleased to find people who are obliging."

He had a newspaper which he spread out on his knees, that no spot might come to his pantaloons, and upon the point of a knife that he always carried in his pocket, he took up a leg all glistening with jelly, put it between his teeth and masticated it with a satisfaction so evident that there ran through the carriage a great sigh of distress.

Then Ball-of-Fat, in a sweet and humble voice, proposed that the two sisters partake of her collation. They both accepted instantly and, without raising their eyes, began to eat very quickly, after stammering their thanks. Cornudet no longer refused the offers of his neighbor, and they formed with the sisters a sort of table, by spreading out some newspapers upon their knees.

The mouths opened and shut without ceasing, they masticated, swallowed, gulping ferociously. Loiseau in his corner was working hard and, in a low voice, was trying to induce his wife to follow his example. She resisted for a long time; then, when a drawn sensation ran through her body, she yielded. Her husband, rounding his phrase, asked their "charming companion" if he might be allowed to offer a little piece to Madame Loiseau.

She replied: "Why, yes, certainly, sir," with an amiable smile, as she passed the dish.

An embarrassing thing confronted them when they opened the first bottle of Bordeaux: they had but one cup. Each passed it after having tasted. Cornudet alone, for politeness without doubt, placed his lips at the spot left humid by his fair neighbor.

Then, surrounded by people eating, suffocated by the odors of the food, the Count and Countess de Breville, as well as Madame and M. Carré-Lamadon, were suffering that odious torment which has preserved the name of Tantalus. Suddenly the young wife of the manufacturer gave forth such a sigh that all heads were turned in her direction; she was as white as the snow without; her eyes closed, her head drooped; she had lost consciousness. Her husband, much excited, implored the help of everybody. Each lost his head completely, until the elder of the two sisters, holding the head of the sufferer, slipped Ball-of-Fat's cup between her lips and forced her to swallow a few drops of wine. The pretty little lady revived, opened her eyes, smiled, and declared in a dying voice that she felt very well now. But, in order that the attack might not return, the sister urged her to drink a full glass of Bordeaux, and added: "It is just hunger, nothing more."

Then Ball-of-Fat, blushing and embarrassed, looked at the four travelers who had fasted and stammered: "Goodness knows! if I dared to offer anything to these gentlemen and ladies, I would—" Then she was silent, as if fearing an insult. Loiseau took up the word: "Ah! certainly, in times like these all the world are brothers and ought to aid each other. Come, ladies, without ceremony; why the devil not accept? We do not know whether we shall even find a house where we can pass the night. At the pace we are going now, we shall not reach Tôtes before noon to-morrow—"

They still hesitated, no one daring to assume the responsibility of a "Yes." The Count decided the question. He turned toward the fat, intimidated girl and, taking on a grand air of condescension, he said to her: "We accept with gratitude, Madame."

It is the first step that counts. The Rubicon passed, one lends himself to the occasion squarely. The basket was stripped. It still contained a *pâté de foie gras*, a *pâté* of larks, a piece of smoked tongue, some preserved pears, a loaf of hard bread, some wafers, and a full cup of pickled gherkins and onions, of which condiments Ball-of-Fat, like all women, was extremely fond.

They could not eat this girl's provisions without speaking to her. And so they chatted, with reserve at first; then, as she carried herself well, with more abandon. The ladies De Breville and Carré-Lamadon, who were acquainted with all the ins and outs of good-breeding, were gracious with a certain delicacy. The Countess, especially, showed that amiable condescension of very noble ladies who do not fear being spoiled by contact with anyone, and was charming. But the great Madame Loiseau, who had the soul of a plebian, remained crabbed, saying little and eating much.

The conversation was about the war, naturally. They related the horrible deeds of the Prussians, the brave acts of the French; and all of them, although running away, did homage to those who stayed behind. Then personal stories began to be told, and Ball-of-Fat related, with sincere emotion, and in the heated words that such girls sometimes use in expressing their natural feelings, how she had left Rouen:

"I believed at first that I could remain," she said. "I had my house full of provisions, and I preferred to feed a few soldiers rather than expatriate myself, to go I knew not where. But as soon as I saw them, those Prussians, that was too much for me! They made my blood boil with anger, and I wept for very shame all day long. Oh! if I were only a man! I watched them from my windows, the great porkers with their pointed helmets, and my maid held my hands to keep me from throwing the furniture down upon them. Then one of them came to lodge at my house; I sprang at his throat the first thing; they are no more difficult to strangle than other people. And I should have put an end to that one then and there had they not pulled me away by the hair. After that, it was necessary to keep out of sight. And finally, when I found an opportunity, I left town and—here I am!"

They congratulated her. She grew in the estimation of her companions, who had not shown themselves so hot-brained, and Cornudet, while listening to her, took on the approving, benevolent smile of an apostle, as a priest would if he heard a devotee praise God, for the long-bearded democrats have a monopoly of patriotism, as the men in cassocks have of religion. In his turn he spoke, in a doctrinal tone, with the emphasis of a proclamation such as we see pasted on the walls about town, and finished by a bit of eloquence whereby he gave that "scamp of a Badinguet" a good lashing.

Then Ball-of-Fat was angry, for she was a Bonapartist. She grew redder than a cherry and, stammering with indignation, said:

"I would like to have seen you in his place, you other people. Then everything would have been quite right; oh, yes! It is you who have betrayed this man! One would never have had to leave France if it had been governed by blackguards like you!"

Cornudet, undisturbed, preserved a disdainful, superior smile, but all felt that the high note had been struck, until the Count, not without some difficulty, calmed the exasperated girl and proclaimed with a manner of authority that all sincere opinions should be respected. But the Countess and the manufacturer's wife, who had in their souls an unreasonable hatred for the people that favor a Republic, and the same instinctive tenderness that all women have for a decorative, despotic government, felt themselves drawn, in spite of themselves, toward this prostitute so full of dignity, whose sentiments so strongly resembled their own.

The basket was empty. By ten o'clock they had easily exhausted the contents and regretted that there was not more. Conversation continued for some time, but a little more coldly since they had finished eating.

The night fell, the darkness little by little became profound, and the cold, felt more during digestion, made Ball-of-Fat shiver in spite of her plumpness. Then Madame de Breville offered her the little footstove, in which the fuel had been renewed many times since morning; she accepted it immediately, for her feet were becoming numb with cold. The ladies Carré-Lamadon and Loiseau gave theirs to the two religious sisters.

The driver had lighted his lanterns. They shone out with a lively glimmer showing a cloud of foam beyond, the sweat of the horses; and, on both sides of the way, the snow seemed to roll itself along under the moving reflection of the lights.

Inside the carriage one could distinguish nothing. But a sudden movement seemed to be made between Ball-of-Fat and Cornudet; and Loiseau, whose eye penetrated the shadow, believed that he saw the big-bearded man start back quickly as if he had received a swift, noiseless blow.

Then some twinkling points of fire appeared in the distance along the road. It was Tôtes. They had traveled eleven hours, which, with the two hours given to resting and feeding the horses, made thirteen. They entered the town and stopped before the Hotel of Commerce.

The carriage door opened! A well-known sound gave the travelers a start; it was the scabbard of a sword hitting the ground. Immediately a German voice was heard in the darkness.

Although the diligence was not moving, no one offered to alight, fearing some one might be waiting to murder them as they stepped out. Then the driver appeared, holding in his hand one of the lanterns which lighted the carriage to its depth, and showed the two rows of frightened faces, whose mouths were open and whose eyes were wide with surprise and fear.

Outside beside the driver, in plain sight, stood a German officer, an excessively tall young man, thin and blond, squeezed into his uniform like a girl in a corset, and wearing on his head a flat, oilcloth cap which made him resemble the porter of an English hotel. His enormous mustache, of long straight hairs, growing gradually thin at each side and terminating in a single blond thread so fine that one could not perceive where it ended, seemed to weigh heavily on the corners of his mouth and, drawing down the cheeks, left a decided wrinkle about the lips.

In Alsatian French, he invited the travelers to come in, saying in a suave tone: "Will you descend, gentlemen and ladies?"

The two good sisters were the first to obey, with the docility of saints accustomed ever to submission. The Count and Countess then appeared, followed by the manufacturer and his wife; then Loiseau, pushing ahead of him his larger half. The last-named, as he set foot on the earth, said to the officer: "Good evening, sir," more as a measure of prudence than politeness. The officer, insolent as all powerful people usually are, looked at him without a word.

Ball-of-Fat and Cornudet, although nearest the door, were the last to descend, grave and haughty before the enemy. The fat girl tried to control herself and be calm. The democrat waved a tragic hand and his long beard seemed to tremble a little and grow redder. They wished to preserve their dignity, comprehending that in such meetings as these they represented in some degree their great country, and somewhat disgusted with the docility of her companions, the fat girl tried to show more pride than her neighbors, the honest women, and, as she felt that some one should set an example, she continued her attitude of resistance assumed at the beginning of the journey.

They entered the vast kitchen of the inn, and the German, having demanded their traveling papers signed by the General-in-chief (in which the name, the description, and profession of each traveler was mentioned), and having examined them all critically, comparing the people and their signatures, said: "It is quite right," and went out.

Then they breathed. They were still hungry and supper was ordered. A half hour was necessary to prepare it, and while two servants were attending to this they went to their rooms. They found them along a corridor which terminated in a large glazed door.

Finally, they sat down at table, when the proprietor of the inn himself appeared. He was a former horse merchant, a large, asthmatic man, with a constant wheezing and rattling in his throat. His father had left him the name of Follenvie. He asked:

"Is Miss Elizabeth Rousset here?"

Ball-of-Fat started as she answered: "It is I."

"The Prussian officer wishes to speak with you immediately."

"With me?"

"Yes, that is, if you are Miss Elizabeth Rousset."

She was disturbed, and reflecting for an instant, declared flatly:

"That is my name, but I shall not go."

A stir was felt around her; each discussed and tried to think of the cause of this order. The Count approached her, saying:

"You are wrong, Madame, for your refusal may lead to considerable difficulty, not only for yourself, but for all your companions. It is never worth while to resist those in power. This request cannot assuredly bring any danger; it is, without doubt, about some forgotten formality."

Everybody agreed with him, asking, begging, beseeching her to go, and at last they convinced her that it was best; they all feared the complications that might result from disobedience. She finally said:

"It is for you that I do this, you understand."

The Countess took her by the hand, saying: "And we are grateful to you for it."

She went out. They waited before sitting down at table.

Each one regretted not having been sent for in the place of this violent, irascible girl, and mentally prepared some platitudes, in case they should be called in their turn.

But at the end of ten minutes she reappeared, out of breath, red to suffocation, and exasperated. She stammered: "Oh! the rascal; the rascal!"

All gathered around to learn something, but she said nothing; and when the Count insisted, she responded with great dignity: "No, it does not concern you; I can say nothing."

Then they all seated themselves around a high soup tureen, whence came the odor of cabbage. In spite of alarm, the supper was gay. The cider was good, the beverage Loiseau and the good sisters took as a means of economy. The others called for wine; Cornudet demanded beer. He had a special fashion of uncorking the bottle, making froth on the liquid, carefully filling the glass and then holding it before the light to better appreciate the color. When he drank, his great beard, which still kept some of the foam of his beloved beverage, seemed to tremble with tenderness; his eyes were squinted, in order not to lose sight of his tipple, and he had the unique air of fulfilling the function for which he was born. One would say that there was in his mind a meeting, like that of affinities, between the two great passions that occupied his life—Pale Ale and Revolutions; and assuredly he could not taste the one without thinking of the other.

Mr. and Mrs. Follenvie dined at the end of the table. The man, rattling like a cracked locomotive, had too much trouble in breathing to talk while eating, but his wife was never silent. She told all her impressions at the arrival of the Prussians, what they did, what they said, reviling them because they cost her some money, and because she had two sons in the army. She addressed herself especially to the Countess, flattered by being able to talk with a lady of quality.

When she lowered her voice to say some delicate thing, her husband would interrupt, from time to time, with: "You had better keep silent, Madame Follenvie." But she paid no attention, continuing in this fashion:

"Yes, Madame, those people there not only eat our potatoes and pork, but our pork and potatoes. And it must not be believed that they are at all proper—oh, no! such filthy things they do, saving the respect I owe to you! And if you could see them exercise for hours in the day! they are all there in the field, marching ahead, then marching back, turning here and turning there. They might be cultivating the land, or at least working on the roads of their own country! But no, Madame, these military men are profitable to no one. Poor people have to feed them, or perhaps be murdered! I am only an old woman without education, it is true, but when I see some endangering their constitutions by raging from morning to night, I say: "When there are so many people found to be useless, how unnecessary it is for others to take so much trouble to be nuisances! Truly, is it not an abomination to kill people, whether they be Prussian, or English, or Polish, or French? If one man revenges himself upon another who has done him some injury, it is wicked and he is punished; but when they exterminate our boys, as if they were game, with guns, they give decorations, indeed, to the one who destroys the most! Now, you see, I can never understand that, never!"

Cornudet raised his voice: "War is a barbarity when one attacks a peaceable neighbor, but a sacred duty when one defends his country."

The old woman lowered her head:

"Yes, when one defends himself, it is another thing; but why not make it a duty to kill all the kings who make these wars for their pleasure?"

Cornudet's eyes flashed. "Bravo, my country-woman!" said he.

Mr. Carré-Lamadon reflected profoundly. Although he was prejudiced as a Captain of Industry, the good sense of this peasant woman made him think of the opulence that would be brought into the country were the idle and consequently mischievous hands, and the troops which were now maintained in unproductiveness, employed in some great industrial work that it would require centuries to achieve.

Loiseau, leaving his place, went to speak with the innkeeper in a low tone of voice. The great man laughed, shook, and squeaked, his corpulence quivered with joy at the jokes of his neighbor, and he bought of him six cases of wine for spring, after the Prussians had gone.

As soon as supper was finished, as they were worn out with fatigue, they retired.

However, Loiseau, who had observed things, after getting his wife to bed, glued his eye and then his ear to a hole in the wall, to try and discover what are known as "the mysteries of the corridor."

At the end of about an hour, he heard a groping, and, looking quickly, he perceived Ball-of-Fat, who appeared still more plump in a blue cashmere negligee trimmed with white lace. She had a candle in her hand and was directing her steps toward the great door at the end of the corridor. But a door at the side opened, and when she returned at the end of some minutes Cornudet, in his suspenders, followed her. They spoke low, then they stopped. Ball-of-Fat seemed to be defending the entrance to her room with energy. Loiseau, unfortunately, could not hear all their words, but finally, as they raised their voices, he was able to catch a few. Cornudet insisted with vivacity. He said:

"Come, now, you are a silly woman; what harm can be done?"

She had an indignant air in responding: "No, my dear, there are moments when such things are out of place. Here it would be a shame."

He doubtless did not comprehend and asked why. Then she cried out, raising her voice still more:

"Why? you do not see why? When there are Prussians in the house, in the very next room, perhaps?"

He was silent. This patriotic shame of the harlot, who would not suffer his caress so near the enemy, must have awakened the latent dignity in his heart, for after simply kissing her, he went back to his own door with a bound.

Loiseau, much excited, left the aperture, cut a caper in his room, put on his pajamas, turned back the clothes that covered the bony carcass of his companion, whom he awakened with a kiss, murmuring: "Do you love me, dearie?"

Then all the house was still. And immediately there arose somewhere, from an uncertain quarter, which might be the cellar but was quite as likely to be the garret, a powerful snoring, monotonous and regular, a heavy, prolonged sound, like a great kettle under pressure. Mr. Follenvie was asleep.

As they had decided that they would set out at eight o'clock the next morning, they all collected in the kitchen. But the carriage, the roof of which was covered with snow, stood undisturbed in the courtyard, without horses and without a driver. They sought him in vain in the stables, in the hay, and in the coach-house. Then they resolved to scour the town, and started out. They found themselves in a square, with a church at one end and some low houses on either side, where they perceived some Prussian soldiers. The first one they saw was paring potatoes. The second, further off, was cleaning the hairdresser's shop. Another, bearded to the eyes, was tending a troublesome brat, cradling it and trying to appease it; and the great peasant women, whose husbands were "away in the army," indicated by signs to their obedient conquerors the work they wished to have done: cutting wood, cooking the soup, grinding the coffee, or what not. One of them even washed the linen of his hostess, an impotent old grandmother.

The Count, astonished, asked questions of the beadle who came out of the rectory. The old man responded:

"Oh! those men are not wicked; they are not the Prussians we hear about. They are from far off, I know not where; and they have left wives and children in their country; it is not amusing to them, this war, I can tell you! I am sure they also weep for their homes, and that it makes as much sorrow among them as it does among us. Here, now, there is not so much unhappiness for the moment, because the soldiers do no harm and they work as if they were in their own homes. You see, sir, among poor people it is necessary that they aid one another. These are the great traits which war develops."

Cornudet, indignant at the cordial relations between the conquerors and the conquered, preferred to shut himself up in the inn. Loiseau had a joke for the occasion: "They will repeople the land."

Mr. Carré-Lamadon had a serious word: "They try to make amends."

But they did not find the driver. Finally, they discovered him in a *café* of the village, sitting at table fraternally with the officer of ordinance. The Count called out to him:

"Were you not ordered to be ready at eight o'clock?"

"Well, yes; but another order has been given me since."

"By whom?"

"Faith! the Prussian commander."

"What was it?"

"Not to harness at all."

"Why?"

"I know nothing about it. Go and ask him. They tell me not to harness, and I don't harness. That's all."

"Did he give you the order himself?"

"No, sir, the innkeeper gave the order for him."

"When was that?"

"Last evening, as I was going to bed."

The three men returned, much disturbed. They asked for Mr. Follenvie, but the servant answered that that gentleman, because of his asthma, never rose before ten o'clock. And he had given strict orders not to be wakened before that, except in case of fire.

They wished to see the officer, but that was absolutely impossible, since, while he lodged at the inn, Mr. Follenvie alone was authorized to speak to him upon civil affairs. So they waited. The women went up to their rooms again and occupied themselves with futile tasks.

Cornudet installed himself near the great chimney in the kitchen, where there was a good fire burning. He ordered one of the little tables to be brought from the *café*, then a can of beer, he then drew out his pipe, which plays among democrats a part almost equal to his own, because in serving Cornudet it was serving its country. It was a superb pipe, an admirably colored meerschaum, as black as the teeth of its master, but perfumed, curved, glistening, easy to the hand, completing his physiognomy. And he remained motionless, his eyes as much fixed upon the flame of the fire as upon his favorite tipple and its frothy crown; and each time that he drank, he passed his long, thin fingers through his scanty, gray hair, with an air of satisfaction, after which he sucked in his mustache fringed with foam.

Loiseau, under the pretext of stretching his legs, went to place some wine among the retailers of the country. The Count and the manufacturer began to talk politics. They could foresee the future of France. One of them believed in an Orléans, the other in some unknown savior for the country, a hero who would reveal himself when all were in despair: a Guesclin, or a Joan of Arc, perhaps, or would it be another Napoleon First? Ah! if the Prince Imperial were not so young!

Cornudet listened to them and smiled like one who holds the word of destiny. His pipe perfumed the kitchen.

As ten o'clock struck, Mr. Follenvie appeared. They asked him hurried questions; but he could only repeat two or three times without variation, these words:

"The officer said to me: 'Mr. Follenvie, you see to it that the carriage is not harnessed for those travelers tomorrow. I do not wish them to leave without my order. That is sufficient.'"

Then they wished to see the officer. The Count sent him his card, on which Mr. Carré-Lamadon wrote his name and all his titles. The Prussian sent back word that he would meet the two gentlemen after he had breakfasted, that is to say, about one o'clock.

The ladies reappeared and ate a little something, despite their disquiet. Ball-of-Fat seemed ill and prodigiously troubled.

They were finishing their coffee when the word came that the officer was ready to meet the gentlemen. Loiseau joined them; but when they tried to enlist Cornudet, to give more solemnity to their proceedings, he declared proudly that he would have nothing to do with the Germans; and he betook himself to his chimney corner and ordered another liter of beer.

The three men mounted the staircase and were introduced to the best room of the inn, where the officer received them, stretched out in an armchair, his feet on the mantelpiece, smoking a long, porcelain pipe, and enveloped in a flamboyant dressing-gown, appropriated, without doubt, from some dwelling belonging to a common citizen of bad taste. He did not rise, nor greet them in any way, not even looking at them. It was a magnificent display of natural blackguardism transformed into the military victor.

At the expiration of some moments, he asked: "What is it you wish?"

The Count became spokesman: "We desire to go on our way, sir."

"No."

"May I ask the cause of this refusal?"

"Because I do not wish it."

"But, I would respectfully observe to you, sir, that your General-in-chief gave us permission to go to Dieppe; and I know of nothing we have done to merit your severity."

"I do not wish it—that is all; you can go."

All three having bowed, retired.

The afternoon was lamentable. They could not understand this caprice of the German; and the most singular ideas would come into their heads to trouble them. Everybody stayed in the kitchen and discussed the situation endlessly, imagining all sorts of unlikely things. Perhaps they would be retained as hostages—but to what end?—or taken prisoners—or rather a considerable ransom might be demanded. At this thought a panic prevailed. The richest were the most frightened, already seeing themselves constrained to pay for their lives with sacks of gold poured into the hands of this insolent soldier. They racked their brains to think of some acceptable falsehoods to conceal their riches and make them pass themselves off for poor people, very poor people. Loiseau took off the chain to his watch and hid it away in his pocket. The falling night increased their apprehensions. The lamp was lighted, and as there was still two hours before dinner, Madame Loiseau proposed a game of Thirty-one. It would be a diversion. They accepted. Cornudet himself, having smoked out his pipe, took part for politeness.

The Count shuffled the cards, dealt, and Ball-of-Fat had thirty-one at the outset; and immediately the interest was great enough to appease the fear that haunted their minds. Then Cornudet perceived that the house of Loiseau was given to tricks.

As they were going to the dinner table, Mr. Follenvie again appeared, and, in wheezing, rattling voice, announced:

"The Prussian officer orders me to ask Miss Elizabeth Rousset if she has yet changed her mind."

Ball-of-Fat remained standing and was pale; then suddenly becoming crimson, such a stifling anger took possession of her that she could not speak. But finally she flashed out: "You may say to the dirty beast, that idiot, that carrion of a Prussian, that I shall never change it; you understand, never, never, never!"

The great innkeeper went out. Then Ball-of-Fat was immediately surrounded, questioned, and solicited by all to disclose the mystery of his visit. She resisted, at first, but soon becoming exasperated, she said: "What does he want? You really want to know what he wants? He wants to sleep with me."

Everybody was choked for words, and indignation was rife. Cornudet broke his glass, so violently did he bring his fist down upon the table. There was a clamor of censure against this ignoble soldier, a blast of anger, a union of all for resistance, as if a demand had been made on each one of the party for the sacrifice exacted of her. The Count declared with disgust that those people conducted themselves after the fashion of the ancient barbarians. The women, especially, showed to Ball-of-Fat a most energetic and tender commiseration. The good sisters who only showed themselves at mealtime, lowered their heads and said nothing.

They all dined, nevertheless, when the first *furore* had abated. But there was little conversation; they were thinking.

The ladies retired early, and the men, all smoking, organized a game at cards to which Mr. Follenvie was invited, as they intended to put a few casual questions to him on the subject of conquering the resistance of this officer. But he thought of nothing but the cards and, without listening or answering, would keep repeating: "To the game, sirs, to the game." His attention was so taken that he even forgot to expectorate, which must have put him some points to the good with the organ in his breast. His whistling lungs ran the whole asthmatic scale, from deep, profound tones to the sharp rustiness of a young cock essaying to crow.

He even refused to retire when his wife, who had fallen asleep previously, came to look for him. She went away alone, for she was an "early bird," always up with the sun, while her husband was a "night owl," always ready to pass the night with his friends. He cried out to her: "Leave my creamed chicken before the fire!" and then went on with his game. When they saw that they could get nothing from him, they declared that it was time to stop, and each sought his bed.

They all rose rather early the next day, with an undefined hope of getting away, which desire the terror of passing another day in that horrible inn greatly increased.

Alas! the horses remained in the stable and the driver was invisible. For want of better employment, they went out and walked around the carriage.

The breakfast was very doleful; and it became apparent that a coldness had arisen toward Ball-of-Fat, and that the night, which brings counsel, had slightly modified their judgments. They almost wished now that the Prussian had secretly found this girl, in order to give her companions a pleasant surprise in the morning. What could be more simple? Besides, who would know anything about it? She could save appearances by telling the officer that she took pity on their distress. To her, it would make so little difference!

No one had avowed these thoughts yet.

In the afternoon, as they were almost perishing from *ennui*, the Count proposed that they take a walk around the village. Each wrapped up warmly and the little party set out, with the exception of Cornudet, who preferred to remain near the fire, and the good sisters, who passed their time in the church or at the curate's.

The cold, growing more intense every day, cruelly pinched their noses and ears; their feet became so numb that each step was torture; and when they came to a field it seemed to them frightfully sad under this limitless white, so that everybody returned immediately, with hearts hard pressed and souls congealed.

The four women walked ahead, the three gentlemen followed just behind. Loiseau, who understood the situation, asked suddenly if they thought that girl there was going to keep them long in such a place as this. The Count, always courteous, said that they could not exact from a woman a sacrifice so hard, unless it should come of her own will. Mr. Carré-Lamadon remarked that if the French made their return through Dieppe, as they were likely to, a battle would surely take place at Tôtes. This reflection made the two others anxious.

"If we could only get away on foot," said Loiseau.

The Count shrugged his shoulders: "How can we think of it in this snow? and with our wives?" he said. "And then, we should be pursued and caught in ten minutes and led back prisoners at the mercy of these soldiers."

It was true, and they were silent.

The ladies talked of their clothes, but a certain constraint seemed to disunite them. Suddenly at the end of the street, the officer appeared. His tall, wasp-like figure in uniform was outlined upon the horizon formed by the snow, and he was marching with knees apart, a gait particularly military, which is affected that they may not spot their carefully blackened boots.

He bowed in passing near the ladies and looked disdainfully at the men, who preserved their dignity by not seeing him, except Loiseau, who made a motion toward raising his hat.

Ball-of-Fat reddened to the ears, and the three married women resented the great humiliation of being thus met by this soldier in the company of this girl whom he had treated so cavalierly.

But they spoke of him, of his figure and his face. Madame Carré-Lamadon, who had known many officers and considered herself a connoisseur of them, found this one not at all bad; she regretted even that he was not French, because he would make such a pretty hussar, one all the women would rave over.

Again in the house, no one knew what to do. Some sharp words, even, were said about things very insignificant. The dinner was silent, and almost immediately after it, each one went to his room to kill time in sleep.

They descended the next morning with weary faces and exasperated hearts. The women scarcely spoke to Ball-of-Fat.

A bell began to ring. It was for a baptism. The fat girl had a child being brought up among the peasants of Yvetot. She had not seen it for a year, or thought of it; but now the idea of a child being baptized threw into her heart a sudden and violent tenderness for her own, and she strongly wished to be present at the ceremony.

As soon as she was gone, everybody looked at each other, then pulled their chairs together, for they thought that finally something should be decided upon. Loiseau had an inspiration: it was to hold Ball-of-Fat alone and let the others go.

Mr. Follenvie was charged with the commission, but he returned almost immediately, for the German, who understood human nature, had put him out. He pretended that he would retain everybody so long as his desire was not satisfied.

Then the commonplace nature of Mrs. Loiseau burst out with:

"Well, we are not going to stay here to die of old age. Since it is the trade of this creature to accommodate herself to all kinds, I fail to see how she has the right to refuse one more than another. I can tell you she has received all she could find in Rouen, even the coachmen! Yes, Madame, the prefect's coachman! I know him very well, for he bought his wine at our house. And to think that to-day we should be drawn into this embarrassment by this affected woman, this minx! For my part, I find that this officer conducts himself very well. He has perhaps suffered privations for a long time; and doubtless he would have preferred us three; but no, he is contented with common property. He respects married women. And we must remember too that he is master. He has only to say 'I wish,' and he could take us by force with his soldiers."

The two women had a cold shiver. Pretty Mrs. Carré-Lamadon's eyes grew brilliant and she became a little pale, as if she saw herself already taken by force by the officer.

The men met and discussed the situation. Loiseau, furious, was for delivering "the wretch" bound hand and foot to the enemy. But the Count, descended through three generations of ambassadors, and endowed with the temperament of a diplomatist, was the advocate of ingenuity.

"It is best to decide upon something," said he. Then they conspired.

The women kept together, the tone of their voices was lowered, each gave advice and the discussion was general. Everything was very harmonious. The ladies especially found delicate shades and charming subtleties of expression for saying the most unusual things. A stranger would have understood nothing, so great was the precaution of language observed. But the light edge of modesty, with which every woman of the world is endowed, only covers the surface; they blossom out in a scandalous adventure of this kind, being deeply amused and feeling themselves in their element, mixing love with sensuality as a greedy cook prepares supper for his master.

Even gaiety returned, so funny did the whole story seem to them at last. The Count found some of the jokes a little off color, but they were so well told that he was forced to smile. In his turn, Loiseau came out with some still bolder tales, and yet nobody was wounded. The brutal thought, expressed by his wife, dominated all minds: "Since it is her trade, why should she refuse this one more than another?" The genteel Mrs. Carré-Lamadon seemed to think that in her place, she would refuse this one less than some others.

They prepared the blockade at length, as if they were about to surround a fortress. Each took some rôle to play, some arguments he would bring to bear, some maneuvers that he would endeavor to put into execution. They decided on the plan of attack, the ruse to employ, the surprise of assault, that should force this living citadel to receive the enemy in her room.

Cornudet remained apart from the rest, and was a stranger to the whole affair.

So entirely were their minds distracted that they did not hear Ball-of-Fat enter. The Count uttered a light "Ssh!" which turned all eyes in her direction. There she was. The abrupt silence and a certain embarrassment hindered them from speaking to her at first. The Countess, more accustomed to the duplicity of society than the others, finally inquired:

"Was it very amusing, that baptism?"

The fat girl, filled with emotion, told them all about it, the faces, the attitudes, and even the appearance of the church. She added: "It is good to pray sometimes."

And up to the time for luncheon these ladies continued to be amiable toward her, in order to increase her docility and her confidence in their counsel. At the table they commenced the approach. This was in the shape of a vague conversation upon devotion. They cited ancient examples: Judith and Holophernes, then, without reason, Lucrece and Sextus, and Cleopatra obliging all the generals of the enemy to pass by her couch and reducing them in servility to slaves. Then they brought out a fantastic story, hatched in the imagination of these ignorant millionaires, where the women of Rome went to Capua for the purpose of lulling Hannibal to sleep in their arms, and his lieutenants and phalanxes of mercenaries as well. They cited all the women who have been taken by conquering armies, making a battlefield of their bodies, making them also a weapon, and a means of success; and all those hideous and detestable beings who have conquered by their heroic caresses, and sacrificed their chastity to vengeance or a beloved cause. They even spoke in veiled terms of that great English family which allowed one of its women to be inoculated with a horrible and contagious disease in order to transmit it to Bonaparte, who was miraculously saved by a sudden illness at the hour of the fatal rendezvous.

And all this was related in an agreeable, temperate fashion, except as it was enlivened by the enthusiasm deemed proper to excite emulation.

One might finally have believed that the sole duty of woman here below was a sacrifice of her person, and a continual abandonment to soldierly caprices.

The two good sisters seemed not to hear, lost as they were in profound thought. Ball-of-Fat said nothing.

During the whole afternoon they let her reflect. But, in the place of calling her "Madame" as they had up to this time, they simply called her "Mademoiselle" without knowing exactly why, as if they had a desire to put her down a degree in their esteem, which she had taken by storm, and make her feel her shameful situation.

The moment supper was served, Mr. Follenvie appeared with his old phrase: "The Prussian officer orders me to ask if Miss Elizabeth Rousset has yet changed her mind."

Ball-of-Fat responded dryly: "No, sir."

But at dinner the coalition weakened. Loiseau made three unhappy remarks. Each one beat his wits for new examples but found nothing; when the Countess, without premeditation, perhaps feeling some vague need of rendering homage to religion, asked the elder of the good sisters to tell them some great deeds in the lives of the saints. It appeared that many of their acts would have been considered crimes in our eyes; but the Church gave absolution of them readily, since they were done for the glory of God, or for the good of all. It was a powerful argument; the Countess made the most of it.

Thus it may be by one of those tacit understandings, or the veiled complacency in which anyone who wears the ecclesiastical garb excels, it may be simply from the effect of a happy unintelligence, a helpful stupidity, but in fact the religious sister lent a formidable support to the conspiracy. They had thought her timid, but she showed herself courageous, verbose, even violent. She was not troubled by the chatter of the casuist; her doctrine seemed a bar of iron; her faith never hesitated; her conscience had no scruples. She found the sacrifice of Abraham perfectly simple, for she would immediately kill father or mother on an order from on high. And nothing, in her opinion, could displease the Lord, if the intention was laudable. The Countess put to use the authority of her unwitting accomplice, and added to it the edifying paraphrase and axiom of Jesuit morals: "The need justifies the means."

Then she asked her: "Then, my sister, do you think that God accepts intentions, and pardons the deed when the motive is pure?"

"Who could doubt it, Madame? Any action blamable in itself often becomes meritorious by the thought it springs from."

And they continued thus, unraveling the will of God, foreseeing his decisions, making themselves interested in things that, in truth, they would never think of noticing. All this was guarded, skillful, discreet. But each word of the saintly sister in a cap helped to break down the resistance of the unworthy courtesan. Then the conversation changed a little, the woman of the chaplet speaking of the houses of her order, of her Superior, of herself, of her dainty neighbor, the dear sister Saint-Nicephore. They had been called to the hospitals of Havre to care for the hundreds of soldiers stricken with smallpox. They depicted these miserable creatures, giving details of the malady. And while they were stopped, *en route*, by the caprice of this Prussian officer, a great number of Frenchmen might die, whom perhaps they could have saved! It was a specialty with her, caring for soldiers. She had been in Crimea, in Italy, in Austria, and, in telling of her campaigns, she revealed herself as one of those religious aids to drums and trumpets, who seem made to follow camps, pick up the wounded in the thick of battle, and, better than an officer, subdue with a word great bands of undisciplined recruits. A true, good sister of the rataplan, whose ravaged face, marked with innumerable scars, appeared the image of the devastation of war.

No one could speak after her, so excellent seemed the effect of her words.

As soon as the repast was ended they quickly went up to their rooms, with the purpose of not coming down the next day until late in the morning.

The luncheon was quiet. They had given the grain of seed time to germinate and bear fruit. The Countess proposed that they take a walk in the afternoon. The Count, being agreeably inclined, gave an arm to Ball-of-Fat and walked behind the others with her. He talked to her in a familiar, paternal tone, a little disdainful, after the manner of men having girls in their employ, calling her "my dear child," from the height of his social position, of his undisputed honor. He reached the vital part of the question at once:

"Then you prefer to leave us here, exposed to the violences which follow a defeat, rather than consent to a favor which you have so often given in your life?"

Ball-of-Fat answered nothing.

Then he tried to reach her through gentleness, reason, and then the sentiments. He knew how to remain "The Count," even while showing himself gallant or complimentary, or very amiable if it became necessary. He exalted the service that she would render them, and spoke of her appreciation; then suddenly became gaily familiar, and said:

"And you know, my dear, it would be something for him to boast of that he had known a pretty girl; something it is difficult to find in his country."

Ball-of-Fat did not answer but joined the rest of the party. As soon as they entered the house she went to her room and did not appear again. The disquiet was extreme. What were they to do? If she continued to resist, what an embarrassment!

The dinner hour struck. They waited in vain. Mr. Follenvie finally entered and said that Miss Rousset was indisposed, and would not be at the table. Everybody pricked up his ears. The Count went to the innkeeper and said in a low voice:

"Is he in there?"

"Yes."

For convenience, he said nothing to his companions, but made a slight sign with his head. Immediately a great sigh of relief went up from every breast and a light appeared in their faces. Loiseau cried out:

"Holy Christopher! I pay for the champagne, if there is any to be found in the establishment." And Mrs. Loiseau was pained to see the proprietor return with four quart bottles in his hands.

Each one had suddenly become communicative and buoyant. A wanton joy filled their hearts. The Count suddenly perceived that Mrs. Carré-Lamadon was charming, the manufacturer paid compliments to the Countess. The conversation was lively, gay, full of witty touches.

Suddenly Loiseau, with anxious face and hand upraised, called out: "Silence!" Everybody was silent, surprised, already frightened. Then he listened intently and said: "S-s-sh!" his two eyes and his hands raised toward the ceiling, listening, and then continuing, in his natural voice: "All right! All goes well!"

They failed to comprehend at first, but soon all laughed. At the end of a quarter of an hour he began the same farce again, renewing it occasionally during the whole afternoon. And he pretended to call to some one in the story above, giving him advice in a double meaning, drawn from the fountain-head—the mind of a commercial traveler. For some moments he would assume a sad air, breathing in a whisper: "Poor girl!" Then he would murmur between his teeth, with an appearance of rage: "Ugh! That scamp of a Prussian." Sometimes, at a moment when no more was thought about it, he would say, in an affected voice, many times over: "Enough! enough!" and add, as if speaking to himself. "If we could only see her again, it isn't necessary that he should kill her, the wretch!"

Although these jokes were in deplorable taste, they amused all and wounded no one, for indignation, like other things, depends upon its surroundings, and the atmosphere which had been gradually created around them was charged with sensual thoughts.

At the dessert the women themselves made some delicate and discreet allusions. Their eyes glistened; they had drunk much. The Count, who preserved, even in his flights, his grand appearance of gravity, made a comparison, much relished, upon the subject of those wintering at the pole, and the joy of shipwrecked sailors who saw an opening toward the south.

Loiseau suddenly arose, a glass of champagne in his hand, and said: "I drink to our deliverance." Everybody was on his feet; they shouted in agreement. Even the two good sisters consented to touch their lips to the froth of the wine which they had never before tasted. They declared that it tasted like charged lemonade, only much nicer.

Loiseau resumed: "It is unfortunate that we have no piano, for we might make up a quadrille."

Cornudet had not said a word, nor made a gesture; he appeared plunged in very grave thoughts, and made sometimes a furious motion, so that his great beard seemed to wish to free itself. Finally, toward midnight, as they were separating, Loiseau, who was staggering, touched him suddenly on the stomach and said to him in a stammer: "You are not very funny, this evening; you have said nothing, citizen!" Then Cornudet raised his head brusquely and, casting a brilliant, terrible glance around the company, said: "I tell you all that you have been guilty of infamy!" He rose, went to the door, and again repeated: "Infamy, I say!" and disappeared.

This made a coldness at first. Loiseau, interlocutor, was stupefied; but he recovered immediately and laughed heartily as he said: "He is very green, my friends. He is very green." And then, as they did not comprehend, he told them about the "mysteries of the corridor." Then there was a return of gaiety. The women behaved like lunatics. The Count and Mr. Carré-Lamadon wept from the force of their laughter. They could not believe it.

"How is that? Are you sure?"

"I tell you I saw it."

"And she refused—"

"Yes, because the Prussian officer was in the next room."

"Impossible!"

"I swear it!"

The Count was stifled with laughter. The industrial gentleman held his sides with both hands. Loiseau continued:

"And now you understand why he saw nothing funny this evening! No, nothing at all!" And the three started out half ill, suffocated.

They separated. But Mrs. Loiseau, who was of a spiteful nature, remarked to her husband as they were getting into bed, that "that *grisette*" of a little Carré-Lamadon was yellow with envy all the evening. "You know," she continued, "how some women will take to a uniform, whether it be French or Prussian! It is all the same to them! Oh! what a pity!"

And all night, in the darkness of the corridor, there were to be heard light noises, like whisperings and walking in bare feet, and imperceptible creakings. They did not go to sleep until late, that is sure, for there were threads of light shining under the doors for a long time. The champagne had its effect; they say it troubles sleep.

The next day a clear winter's sun made the snow very brilliant. The diligence, already harnessed, waited before the door, while an army of white pigeons, in their thick plumage, with rose-colored eyes, with a black spot in the center, walked up and down gravely among the legs of the six horses, seeking their livelihood in the manure there scattered.

The driver, enveloped in his sheepskin, had a lighted pipe under the seat, and all the travelers, radiant, were rapidly packing some provisions for the rest of the journey. They were only waiting for Ball-of-Fat. Finally she appeared.

She seemed a little troubled, ashamed. And she advanced timidly toward her companions, who all, with one motion, turned as if they had not seen her. The Count, with dignity, took the arm of his wife and removed her from this impure contact.

The fat girl stopped, half stupefied; then, plucking up courage, she approached the manufacturer's wife with "Good morning, Madame," humbly murmured. The lady made a slight bow of the head which she accompanied with a look of outraged virtue. Everybody seemed busy, and kept themselves as far from her as if she had had some infectious disease in her skirts. Then they hurried into the carriage, where she came last, alone, and where she took the place she had occupied during the first part of the journey.

They seemed not to see her or know her; although Madame Loiseau, looking at her from afar, said to her husband in a half-tone: "Happily, I don't have to sit beside her."

The heavy carriage began to move and the remainder of the journey commenced. No one spoke at first. Ball-of-Fat dared not raise her eyes. She felt indignant toward all her neighbors, and at the same time humiliated at having yielded to the foul kisses of this Prussian, into whose arms they had hypocritically thrown her.

Then the Countess, turning toward Mrs. Carré-Lamadon, broke the difficult silence:

"I believe you know Madame d'Etrelles?"

"Yes, she is one of my friends."

"What a charming woman!"

"Delightful! A very gentle nature, and well educated, besides; then she is an artist to the tips of her fingers, sings beautifully, and draws to perfection."

The manufacturer chatted with the Count, and in the midst of the rattling of the glass, an occasional word escaped such as "coupon— premium—limit—expiration."

Loiseau, who had pilfered the old pack of cards from the inn, greasy through five years of contact with tables badly cleaned, began a game of bezique with his wife.

The good sisters took from their belt the long rosary which hung there, made together the sign of the cross, and suddenly began to move their lips in a lively murmur, as if they were going through the whole of the "Oremus." And from time to time they kissed a medal, made the sign anew, then recommenced their muttering, which was rapid and continued.

Cornudet sat motionless, thinking.

At the end of three hours on the way, Loiseau put up the cards and said: "I am hungry."

His wife drew out a package from whence she brought a piece of cold veal. She cut it evenly in thin pieces and they both began to eat.

"Suppose we do the same," said the Countess.

They consented to it and she undid the provisions prepared for the two couples. It was in one of those dishes whose lid is decorated with a china hare, to signify that a *pâté* of hare is inside, a succulent dish of pork, where white rivers of lard cross the brown flesh of the game, mixed with some other viands hashed fine. A beautiful square of Gruyère cheese, wrapped in a piece of newspaper, preserved the imprint "divers things" upon the unctuous plate.

The two good sisters unrolled a big sausage which smelled of garlic; and Cornudet plunged his two hands into the vast pockets of his overcoat, at the same time, and drew out four hard eggs and a piece of bread. He removed the shells and threw them in the straw under his feet; then he began to eat the eggs, letting fall on his vast beard some bits of clear yellow, which looked like stars caught there.

Ball-of-Fat, in the haste and distraction of her rising, had not thought of anything; and she looked at them exasperated, suffocating with rage, at all of them eating so placidly. A tumultuous anger swept over her at first, and she opened her mouth to cry out at them, to hurl at them a flood of injury which mounted to her lips; but she could not speak, her exasperation strangled her.

No one looked at her or thought of her. She felt herself drowned in the scorn of these honest scoundrels, who had first sacrificed her and then rejected her, like some improper or useless article. She thought of her great basket full of good things which they had greedily devoured, of her two chickens shining with jelly, of her *pâtés*, her pears, and the four bottles of Bordeaux; and her fury suddenly falling, as a cord drawn too tightly breaks, she felt ready to weep. She made terrible efforts to prevent it, making ugly faces, swallowing her sobs as children do, but the tears came and glistened in the corners of her eyes, and then two great drops, detaching themselves from the rest, rolled slowly down like little streams of water that filter through rock, and, falling regularly, rebounded upon her breast. She sits erect, her eyes fixed, her face rigid and pale, hoping that no one will notice her.

But the Countess perceives her and tells her husband by a sign. He shrugs his shoulders, as much as to say:

"What would you have me do, it is not my fault."

Mrs. Loiseau indulged in a mute laugh of triumph and murmured:

"She weeps for shame."

The two good sisters began to pray again, after having wrapped in a paper the remainder of their sausage.

Then Cornudet, who was digesting his eggs, extended his legs to the seat opposite, crossed them, folded his arms, smiled like a man who is watching a good farce, and began to whistle the "Marseillaise."

All faces grew dark. The popular song assuredly did not please his neighbors. They became nervous and agitated, having an appearance of wishing to howl, like dogs, when they hear a barrel organ. He perceived this but did not stop. Sometimes he would hum the words:

> "Sacred love of country
> Help, sustain th' avenging arm;
> Liberty, sweet Liberty
> Ever fight, with no alarm."

They traveled fast, the snow being harder. But as far as Dieppe, during the long, sad hours of the journey, across the jolts in the road, through the falling night, in the profound darkness of the carriage, he continued his vengeful, monotonous whistling with a ferocious obstinacy, constraining his neighbors to follow the song from one end to the other, and to recall the words that belonged to each measure.

And Ball-of-Fat wept continually; and sometimes a sob, which she was not able to restrain, echoed between the two rows of people in the shadows.

The Necklace

SHE WAS ONE of those pretty, charming young ladies, born, as if through an error of destiny, into a family of clerks. She had no dowry, no hopes, no means of becoming known, appreciated, loved, and married by a man either rich or distinguished; and she allowed herself to marry a petty clerk in the office of the Board of Education.

She was simple, not being able to adorn herself; but she was unhappy, as one out of her class; for women belong to no caste, no race; their grace, their beauty, and their charm serving them in the place of birth and family. Their inborn finesse, their instinctive elegance, their suppleness of wit are their only aristocracy, making some daughters of the people the equal of great ladies.

She suffered incessantly, feeling herself born for all delicacies and luxuries. She suffered from the poverty of her apartment, the shabby walls, the worn chairs, and the faded stuffs. All these things, which another woman of her station would not have noticed, tortured and angered her. The sight of the little Breton, who made this humble home, awoke in her sad regrets and desperate dreams. She thought of quiet ante-chambers, with their Oriental hangings, lighted by high, bronze torches, and of the two great footmen in short trousers who sleep in the large armchairs, made sleepy by the heavy air from the heating apparatus. She thought of large drawing-rooms, hung in old silks, of graceful pieces of furniture carrying bric-à-brac of inestimable value, and of the little perfumed coquettish apartments, made for five o'clock chats with most intimate friends, men known and sought after, whose attention all women envied and desired.

When she seated herself for dinner, before the round table where the tablecloth had been used three days, opposite her husband who uncovered the tureen with a delighted air, saying: "Oh! the good potpie! I know nothing better than that—" she would think of the elegant dinners, of the shining silver, of the tapestries peopling the walls with ancient personages and rare birds in the midst of fairy forests; she thought of the exquisite food served on marvelous dishes, of the whispered gallantries, listened to with the smile of the sphinx, while eating the rose-colored flesh of the trout or a chicken's wing.

She had neither frocks nor jewels, nothing. And she loved only those things. She felt that she was made for them. She had such a desire to please, to be sought after, to be clever, and courted.

She had a rich friend, a schoolmate at the convent, whom she did not like to visit, she suffered so much when she returned. And she wept for whole days from chagrin, from regret, from despair, and disappointment.

*   *   *

One evening her husband returned elated bearing in his hand a large envelope.

"Here," he said, "here is something for you."

She quickly tore open the wrapper and drew out a printed card on which were inscribed these words:

"The Minister of Public Instruction and Madame George Ramponneau ask the honor of Mr. and Mrs. Loisel's company Monday evening, January 18, at the Minister's residence."

Instead of being delighted, as her husband had hoped, she threw the invitation spitefully upon the table murmuring:

"What do you suppose I want with that?"

"But, my dearie, I thought it would make you happy. You never go out, and this is an occasion, and a fine one! I had a great deal of trouble to get it. Everybody wishes one, and it is very select; not many are given to employees. You will see the whole official world there."

She looked at him with an irritated eye and declared impatiently:

"What do you suppose I have to wear to such a thing as that?"

He had not thought of that; he stammered:

"Why, the dress you wear when we go to the theater. It seems very pretty to me—"

He was silent, stupefied, in dismay, at the sight of his wife weeping. Two great tears fell slowly from the corners of her eyes toward the corners of her mouth; he stammered:

"What is the matter? What is the matter?"

By a violent effort, she had controlled her vexation and responded in a calm voice, wiping her moist cheeks:

"Nothing. Only I have no dress and consequently I cannot go to this affair. Give your card to some colleague whose wife is better fitted out than I."

He was grieved, but answered:

"Let us see, Matilda. How much would a suitable costume cost, something that would serve for other occasions, something very simple?"

She reflected for some seconds, making estimates and thinking of a sum that she could ask for without bringing with it an immediate refusal and a frightened exclamation from the economical clerk.

Finally she said, in a hesitating voice:

"I cannot tell exactly, but it seems to me that four hundred francs ought to cover it."

He turned a little pale, for he had saved just this sum to buy a gun that he might be able to join some hunting parties the next summer, on the plains at Nanterre, with some friends who went to shoot larks up there on Sunday. Nevertheless, he answered:

"Very well. I will give you four hundred francs. But try to have a pretty dress."

*   *   *

The day of the ball approached and Mme. Loisel seemed sad, disturbed, anxious. Nevertheless, her dress was nearly ready. Her husband said to her one evening:

"What is the matter with you? You have acted strangely for two or three days."

And she responded: "I am vexed not to have a jewel, not one stone, nothing to adorn myself with. I shall have such a poverty-laden look. I would prefer not to go to this party."

He replied: "You can wear some natural flowers. At this season they look very *chic*. For ten francs you can have two or three magnificent roses."

She was not convinced. "No," she replied, "there is nothing more humiliating than to have a shabby air in the midst of rich women."

Then her husband cried out: "How stupid we are! Go and find your friend Mrs. Forestier and ask her to lend you her jewels. You are well enough acquainted with her to do this."

She uttered a cry of joy: "It is true!" she said. "I had not thought of that."

The next day she took herself to her friend's house and related her story of distress. Mrs. Forestier went to her closet with the glass doors, took out a large jewel-case, brought it, opened it, and said: "Choose, my dear."

She saw at first some bracelets, then a collar of pearls, then a Venetian cross of gold and jewels and of admirable workmanship. She tried the jewels before the glass, hesitated, but could neither decide to take them nor leave them. Then she asked:

"Have you nothing more?"

"Why, yes. Look for yourself. I do not know what will please you."

Suddenly she discovered, in a black satin box, a superb necklace of diamonds, and her heart beat fast with an immoderate desire. Her hands trembled as she took them up. She placed them about her throat against her dress, and remained in ecstasy before them. Then she asked, in a hesitating voice, full of anxiety:

"Could you lend me this? Only this?"

"Why, yes, certainly."

She fell upon the neck of her friend, embraced her with passion, then went away with her treasure.

*   *   *

The day of the ball arrived. Mme. Loisel was a great success. She was the prettiest of all, elegant, gracious, smiling, and full of joy. All the men noticed her, asked her name, and wanted to be presented. All the members of the Cabinet wished to waltz with her. The Minister of Education paid her some attention.

She danced with enthusiasm, with passion, intoxicated with pleasure, thinking of nothing, in the triumph of her beauty, in the glory of her success, in a kind of cloud of happiness that came of all this homage, and all this admiration, of all these awakened desires, and this victory so complete and sweet to the heart of woman.

She went home toward four o'clock in the morning. Her husband had been half asleep in one of the little salons since midnight, with three other gentlemen whose wives were enjoying themselves very much.

He threw around her shoulders the wraps they had carried for the coming home, modest garments of everyday wear, whose poverty clashed with the elegance of the ball costume. She felt this and wished to hurry away in order not to be noticed by the other women who were wrapping themselves in rich furs.

Loisel retained her: "Wait," said he. "You will catch cold out there. I am going to call a cab."

But she would not listen and descended the steps rapidly. When they were in the street, they found no carriage; and they began to seek for one, hailing the coachmen whom they saw at a distance.

They walked along toward the Seine, hopeless and shivering. Finally they found on the quay one of those old, nocturnal *coupés* that one sees in Paris after nightfall, as if they were ashamed of their misery by day.

It took them as far as their door in Martyr street, and they went wearily up to their apartment. It was all over for her. And on his part, he remembered that he would have to be at the office by ten o'clock.

She removed the wraps from her shoulders before the glass, for a final view of herself in her glory. Suddenly she uttered a cry. Her necklace was not around her neck.

Her husband, already half undressed, asked: "What is the matter?"

She turned toward him excitedly:

"I have—I have—I no longer have Mrs. Forestier's necklace."

He arose in dismay: "What! How is that? It is not possible."

And they looked in the folds of the dress, in the folds of the mantle, in the pockets, everywhere. They could not find it.

He asked: "You are sure you still had it when we left the house?"

"Yes, I felt it in the vestibule as we came out."

"But if you had lost it in the street, we should have heard it fall. It must be in the cab."

"Yes. It is probable. Did you take the number?"

"No. And you, did you notice what it was?"

"No."

They looked at each other utterly cast down. Finally, Loisel dressed himself again.

"I am going," said he, "over the track where we went on foot, to see if I can find it."

And he went. She remained in her evening gown, not having the force to go to bed, stretched upon a chair, without ambition or thoughts.

Toward seven o'clock her husband returned. He had found nothing.

He went to the police and to the cab offices, and put an advertisement in the newspapers, offering a reward; he did everything that afforded them a suspicion of hope.

She waited all day in a state of bewilderment before this frightful disaster. Loisel returned at evening with his face harrowed and pale; and had discovered nothing.

"It will be necessary," said he, "to write to your friends that you have broken the clasp of the necklace and that you will have it repaired. That will give us time to turn around."

She wrote as he dictated.

*   *   *

At the end of a week, they had lost all hope. And Loisel, older by five years, declared:

"We must take measures to replace this jewel."

The next day they took the box which had inclosed it, to the jeweler whose name was on the inside. He consulted his books:

"It is not I, Madame," said he, "who sold this necklace; I only furnished the casket."

Then they went from jeweler to jeweler seeking a necklace like the other one, consulting their memories, and ill, both of them, with chagrin and anxiety.

In a shop of the Palais-Royal, they found a chaplet of diamonds which seemed to them exactly like the one they had lost. It was valued at forty thousand francs. They could get it for thirty-six thousand.

They begged the jeweler not to sell it for three days. And they made an arrangement by which they might return it for thirty-four thousand francs if they found the other one before the end of February.

Loisel possessed eighteen thousand francs which his father had left him. He borrowed the rest.

He borrowed it, asking for a thousand francs of one, five hundred of another, five louis of this one, and three louis of that one. He gave notes, made ruinous promises, took money of usurers and the whole race of lenders. He compromised his whole existence, in fact, risked his signature, without even knowing whether he could make it good or not, and, harassed by anxiety for the future, by the black misery which surrounded him, and by the prospect of all physical privations and moral torture, he went to get the new necklace, depositing on the merchant's counter thirty-six thousand francs.

When Mrs. Loisel took back the jewels to Mrs. Forestier, the latter said to her in a frigid tone:

"You should have returned them to me sooner, for I might have needed them."

She did open the jewel-box as her friend feared she would. If she should perceive the substitution, what would she think? What should she say? Would she take her for a robber?

*   *   *

Mrs. Loisel now knew the horrible life of necessity. She did her part, however, completely, heroically. It was necessary to pay this frightful debt. She would pay it. They sent away the maid; they changed their lodgings; they rented some rooms under a mansard roof.

She learned the heavy cares of a household, the odious work of a kitchen. She washed the dishes, using her rosy nails upon the greasy pots and the bottoms of the stewpans. She washed the soiled linen, the chemises and dishcloths, which she hung on the line to dry; she took down the refuse to the street each morning and brought up the water, stopping at each landing to breathe. And, clothed like a woman of the people, she went to the grocer's, the butcher's, and the fruiterer's, with her basket on her arm, shopping, haggling to the last sou her miserable money.

Every month it was necessary to renew some notes, thus obtaining time, and to pay others.

The husband worked evenings, putting the books of some merchants in order, and nights he often did copying at five sous a page.

And this life lasted for ten years.

At the end of ten years, they had restored all, all, with interest of the usurer, and accumulated interest besides.

Mrs. Loisel seemed old now. She had become a strong, hard woman, the crude woman of the poor household. Her hair badly dressed, her skirts awry, her hands red, she spoke in a loud tone, and washed the floors in large pails of water. But sometimes, when her husband was at the office, she would seat herself before the window and think of that evening party of former times, of that ball where she was so beautiful and so flattered.

How would it have been if she had not lost that necklace? Who knows? Who knows? How singular is life, and how full of changes! How small a thing will ruin or save one!

*   *   *

One Sunday, as she was taking a walk in the Champs-Elysées to rid herself of the cares of the week, she suddenly perceived a woman walking with a child. It was Mrs. Forestier, still young, still pretty, still attractive. Mrs. Loisel was affected. Should she speak to her? Yes, certainly. And now that she had paid, she would tell her all. Why not?

She approached her. "Good morning, Jeanne."

Her friend did not recognize her and was astonished to be so familiarly addressed by this common personage. She stammered:

"But, Madame—I do not know—You must be mistaken—"

"No, I am Matilda Loisel."

Her friend uttered a cry of astonishment: "Oh! my poor Matilda! How you have changed—"

"Yes, I have had some hard days since I saw you; and some miserable ones—and all because of you—"

"Because of me? How is that?"

"You recall the diamond necklace that you loaned me to wear to the Commissioner's ball?"

"Yes, very well."

"Well, I lost it."

"How is that, since you returned it to me?"

"I returned another to you exactly like it. And it has taken us ten years to pay for it. You can understand that it was not easy for us who have nothing. But it is finished and I am decently content."

Madame Forestier stopped short. She said:

"You say that you bought a diamond necklace to replace mine?"

"Yes. You did not perceive it then? They were just alike."

And she smiled with a proud and simple joy. Madame Forestier was touched and took both her hands as she replied:

"Oh! my poor Matilda! Mine were false. They were not worth over five hundred francs!"

A Piece of String

ALONG ALL THE roads around Goderville the peasants and their wives were coming toward the burgh because it was market day. The men were proceeding with slow steps, the whole body bent forward at each movement of their long twisted legs, deformed by their hard work, by the weight on the plow which, at the same time, raised the left shoulder and swerved the figure, by the reaping of the wheat which made the knees spread to make a firm "purchase," by all the slow and painful labors of the country. Their blouses, blue, "stiff-starched," shining as if varnished, ornamented with a little design in white at the neck and wrists, puffed about their bony bodies, seemed like balloons ready to carry them off. From each of them a head, two arms, and two feet protruded.

Some led a cow or a calf by a cord, and their wives, walking behind the animal, whipped its haunches with a leafy branch to hasten its progress. They carried large baskets on their arms from which, in some cases, chickens and, in others, ducks thrust out their heads. And they walked with a quicker, livelier step than their husbands. Their spare straight figures were wrapped in a scanty little shawl, pinned over their flat bosoms, and their heads were enveloped in a white cloth glued to the hair and surmounted by a cap.

Then a wagon passed at the jerky trot of a nag, shaking strangely, two men seated side by side and a woman in the bottom of the vehicle, the latter holding on to the sides to lessen the hard jolts.

In the public square of Goderville there was a crowd, a throng of human beings and animals mixed together. The horns of the cattle, the tall hats with long nap of the rich peasant, and the headgear of the peasant women rose above the surface of the assembly. And the clamorous, shrill, screaming voices made a continuous and savage din which sometimes was dominated by the robust lungs of some countryman's laugh, or the long lowing of a cow tied to the wall of a house.

All that smacked of the stable, the dairy and the dirt heap, hay and sweat, giving forth that unpleasant odor, human and animal, peculiar to the people of the field.

Maître Hauchecome, of Breaute, had just arrived at Goderville, and he was directing his steps toward the public square, when he perceived upon the ground a little piece of string. Maître Hauchecome, economical like a true Norman, thought that everything useful ought to be picked up, and he bent painfully, for he suffered from rheumatism. He took the bit of thin cord from the ground and began to roll it carefully when he noticed Maître Malandain, the harness-maker, on the threshold of his door, looking at him. They had heretofore had business together on the subject of a halter, and they were on bad terms, being both good haters. Maître Hauchecome was seized with a sort of shame to be seen thus by his enemy, picking a bit of string out of the dirt. He concealed his "find" quickly under his blouse, then in his trousers' pocket; then he pretended to be still looking on the ground for something which he did not find, and he went toward the market, his head forward, bent double by his pains.

He was soon lost in the noisy and slowly moving crowd, which was busy with interminable bargainings. The peasants milked, went and came, perplexed, always in fear of being cheated, not daring to decide, watching the vender's eye, ever trying to find the trick in the man and the flaw in the beast.

The women, having placed their great baskets at their feet, had taken out the poultry which lay upon the ground, tied together by the feet, with terrified eyes and scarlet crests.

They heard offers, stated their prices with a dry air and impassive face, or perhaps, suddenly deciding on some proposed reduction, shouted to the customer who was slowly going away: "All right, Maître Authirne, I'll give it to you for that."

Then little by little the square was deserted, and the Angelus ringing at noon, those who had stayed too long, scattered to their shops.

At Jourdain's the great room was full of people eating, as the big court was full of vehicles of all kinds, carts, gigs, wagons, dump carts, yellow with dirt, mended and patched, raising their shafts to the sky like two arms, or perhaps with their shafts in the ground and their backs in the air.

Just opposite the diners seated at the table, the immense fireplace, filled with bright flames, cast a lively heat on the backs of the row on the right. Three spits were turning on which were chickens, pigeons, and legs of mutton; and an appetizing odor of roast beef and gravy dripping over the nicely browned skin rose from the hearth, increased the jovialness, and made everybody's mouth water.

All the aristocracy of the plow ate there, at Maître Jourdain's, tavern keeper and horse dealer, a rascal who had money.

The dishes were passed and emptied, as were the jugs of yellow cider. Everyone told his affairs, his purchases, and sales. They discussed the crops. The weather was favorable for the green things but not for the wheat.

Suddenly the drum beat in the court, before the house. Everybody rose except a few indifferent persons, and ran to the door, or to the windows, their mouths still full and napkins in their hands.

After the public crier had ceased his drum-beating, he called out in a jerky voice, speaking his phrases irregularly:

"It is hereby made known to the inhabitants of Goderville, and in general to all persons present at the market, that there was lost this morning, on the road to Benzeville, between nine and ten o'clock, a black leather pocketbook containing five hundred francs and some business papers. The finder is requested to return same with all haste to the mayor's office or to Maître Fortune Houlbreque of Manneville; there will be twenty francs reward."

Then the man went away. The heavy roll of the drum and the crier's voice were again heard at a distance.

Then they began to talk of this event discussing the chances that Maître Houlbreque had of finding or not finding his pocketbook.

And the meal concluded. They were finishing their coffee when a chief of the gendarmes appeared upon the threshold.

He inquired:

"Is Maître Hauchecome, of Breaute, here?"

Maître Hauchecome, seated at the other end of the table, replied:

"Here I am."

And the officer resumed:

"Maître Hauchecome, will you have the goodness to accompany me to the mayor's office? The mayor would like to talk to you."

The peasant, surprised and disturbed, swallowed at a draught his tiny glass of brandy, rose, and, even more bent than in the morning, for the first steps after each rest were specially difficult, set out, repeating: "Here I am, here I am."

The mayor was awaiting him, seated on an armchair. He was the notary of the vicinity, a stout, serious man, with pompous phrases.

"Maître Hauchecome," said he, "you were seen this morning to pick up, on the road to Benzeville, the pocketbook lost by Maître Houlbreque of Manneville."

The countryman, astounded, looked at the mayor, already terrified, by this suspicion resting on him without his knowing why.

"Me? Me? Me pick up the pocketbook?"

"Yes, you, yourself."

"Word of honor, I never heard of it."

"But you were seen."

"I was seen, me? Who says he saw me?"

"Monsieur Malandain, the harness-maker."

The old man remembered, understood, and flushed with anger.

"Ah, he saw me, the clodhopper, he saw me pick up this string, here, M'sieu the Mayor." And rummaging in his pocket he drew out the little piece of string.

But the mayor, incredulous, shook his head.

"You will not make me believe, Maître Hauchecome, that Monsieur Malandain, who is a man worthy of credence, mistook this cord for a pocketbook."

The peasant, furious, lifted his hand, spat at one side to attest his honor, repeating:

"It is nevertheless the truth of the good God, the sacred truth, M'sieu' the Mayor. I repeat it on my soul and my salvation."

The mayor resumed:

"After picking up the object, you stood like a stilt, looking a long while in the mud to see if any piece of money had fallen out."

The good, old man choked with indignation and fear.

"How anyone can tell—how anyone can tell—such lies to take away an honest man's reputation! How can anyone—"

There was no use in his protesting, nobody believed him. He was confronted with Monsieur Malandain, who repeated and maintained his affirmation. They abused each other for an hour. At his own request, Maître Hauchecome was searched, nothing was found on him.

Finally the mayor, very much perplexed, discharged him with the warning that he would consult the public prosecutor and ask for further orders.

The news had spread. As he left the mayor's office, the old man was surrounded and questioned with a serious or bantering curiosity, in which there was no indignation. He began to tell the story of the string. No one believed him. They laughed at him.

He went along, stopping his friends, beginning endlessly his statement and his protestations, showing his pockets turned inside out, to prove that he had nothing.

They said:

"Old rascal, get out!"

And he grew angry, becoming exasperated, hot, and distressed at not being believed, not knowing what to do and always repeating himself.

Night came. He must depart. He started on his way with three neighbors to whom he pointed out the place where he had picked up the bit of string; and all along the road he spoke of his adventure.

In the evening he took a turn in the village of Breaute, in order to tell it to everybody. He only met with incredulity.

It made him ill at night.

The next day about one o'clock in the afternoon, Marius Paumelle, a hired man in the employ of Maître Breton, husbandman at Ymanville, returned the pocketbook and its contents to Maître Houlbreque of Manneville.

This man claimed to have found the object in the road; but not knowing how to read, he had carried it to the house and given it to his employer.

The news spread through the neighborhood. Maître Hauchecome was informed of it. He immediately went the circuit and began to recount his story completed by the happy climax. He was in triumph.

"What grieved me so much was not the thing itself, as the lying. There is nothing so shameful as to be placed under a cloud on account of a lie."

He talked of his adventure all day long, he told it on the highway to people who were passing by, in the wine-shop to people who were drinking there, and to persons coming out of church the following Sunday. He stopped strangers to tell them about it. He was calm now, and yet something disturbed him without his knowing exactly what it was. People had the air of joking while they listened. They did not seem convinced. He seemed to feel that remarks were being made behind his back.

On Tuesday of the next week he went to the market at Goderville, urged solely by the necessity he felt of discussing the case.

Malandain, standing at his door, began to laugh on seeing him pass. Why?

He approached a farmer from Crequetot, who did not let him finish, and giving him a thump in the stomach said to his face:

"You big rascal."

Then he turned his back on him.

Maître Hauchecome was confused, why was he called a big rascal?

When he was seated at the table in Jourdain's tavern he commenced to explain "the affair."

A horse dealer from Monvilliers called to him:

"Come, come, old sharper, that's an old trick; I know all about your piece of string!"

Hauchecome stammered:

"But since the pocketbook was found."

But the other man replied:

"Shut up, papa, there is one that finds, and there is one that reports. At any rate you are mixed with it."

The peasant stood choking. He understood. They accused him of having had the pocketbook returned by a confederate, by an accomplice.

He tried to protest. All the table began to laugh.

He could not finish his dinner and went away, in the midst of jeers.

He went home ashamed and indignant, choking with anger and confusion, the more dejected that he was capable with his Norman cunning of doing what they had accused him of, and even boasting of it as of a good turn. His innocence to him, in a confused way, was impossible to prove, as his sharpness was known. And he was stricken to the heart by the injustice of the suspicion.

Then he began to recount the adventures again, prolonging his history every day, adding each time, new reasons, more energetic protestations, more solemn oaths which he imagined and prepared in his hours of solitude, his whole mind given up to the story of the string. He was believed so much the less as his defense was more complicated and his arguing more subtle.

"Those are lying excuses," they said behind his back.

He felt it, consumed his heart over it, and wore himself out with useless efforts. He wasted away before their very eyes.

The wags now made him tell about the string to amuse them, as they make a soldier who has been on a campaign tell about his battles. His mind, touched to the depth, began to weaken.

Toward the end of December he took to his bed.

He died in the first days of January, and in the delirium of his death struggles he kept claiming his innocence, reiterating:

"A piece of string, a piece of string,—look—here it is, M'sieu' the Mayor."

Mme. Tellier's Establishment

MEN WENT THERE every evening at about eleven o'clock, just as they went to the *café*. Six or eight of them used to meet there; always the same set, not fast men, but respectable tradesmen, and young men in government or some other employ; and they used to drink their Chartreuse, and tease the girls, or else they would talk seriously with Madame, whom everybody respected, and then would go home at twelve o'clock! The younger men would sometimes stay the night.

It was a small, comfortable house, at the corner of a street behind Saint

Etienne's church. From the windows one could see the docks, full of ships which were being unloaded, and on the hill the old, gray chapel, dedicated to the Virgin.

Madame, who came of a respectable family of peasant proprietors in the department of the Eure, had taken up her profession, just as she would have become a milliner or dressmaker. The prejudice against prostitution, which is so violent and deeply rooted in large towns, does not exist in the country places in Normandy. The peasant simply says: "It is a paying business," and sends his daughter to keep a harem of fast girls, just as he would send her to keep a girls' school.

She had inherited the house from an old uncle, to whom it had belonged. Monsieur and Madame, who had formerly been innkeepers near Yvetot, had immediately sold their house, as they thought that the business at Fécamp was more profitable. They arrived one fine morning to assume the direction of the enterprise, which was declining on account of the absence of a head. They were good people enough in their way, and soon made themselves liked by their staff and their neighbors.

Monsieur died of apoplexy two years later, for as his new profession kept him in idleness and without exercise, he had grown excessively stout, and his health had suffered. Since Madame had been a widow, all the frequenters of the establishment had wanted her; but people said that personally she was quite virtuous, and even the girls in the house could not discover anything against her. She was tall, stout, and affable, and her complexion, which had become pale in the dimness of her house, the shutters of which were scarcely ever opened, shone as if it had been varnished. She had a fringe of curly, false hair, which gave her a juvenile look, which in turn contrasted strongly with her matronly figure. She was always smiling and cheerful, and was fond of a joke, but there was a shade of reserve about her which her new occupation had not quite made her lose. Coarse words always shocked her, and when any young fellow who had been badly brought up called her establishment by its right name, she was angry and disgusted.

In a word, she had a refined mind, and although she treated her women as friends, yet she very frequently used to say that she and they were not made of the same stuff.

Sometimes during the week she would hire a carriage and take some of her girls into the country, where they used to enjoy themselves on the grass by the side of the little river. They behaved like a lot of girls let out from a school, and used to run races, and play childish games. They would have a cold dinner on the grass, and drink cider, and go home at night with a delicious feeling of fatigue, and in the carriage kiss Madame as a kind mother who was full of goodness and complaisance.

The house had two entrances. At the corner there was a sort of low *café*, which sailors and the lower orders frequented at night, and she had two girls whose special duty it was to attend to that part of the business. With the assistance of the waiter, whose name was Frederic, and who was a short, light-haired, beardless fellow, as strong as a horse, they set the half bottles of wine and the jugs of beer on the shaky marble tables and then, sitting astride on the customers' knees, would urge them to drink.

The three other girls (there were only five in all), formed a kind of aristocracy, and were reserved for the company on the first floor, unless they were wanted downstairs, and there was nobody on the first floor. The salon of Jupiter, where the tradesmen used to meet, was papered in blue, and embellished with a large drawing representing Leda stretched out under the swan. That room was reached by a winding staircase, which ended at a narrow door opening on to the street, and above it, all night long a little lamp burned, behind wire bars, such as one still sees in some towns, at the foot of the shrine of some saint.

The house, which was old and damp, rather smelled of mildew. At times there was an odor of eau de Cologne in the passages, or a half-open door downstairs allowed the noise of the common men sitting and drinking downstairs to reach the first floor, much to the disgust of the gentlemen who were there. Madame, who was quite familiar with those of her customers with whom she was on friendly terms, did not leave the salon. She took much interest in what was going on in the town, and they regularly told her all the news. Her serious conversation was a change from the ceaseless chatter of the three women; it was a rest from the doubtful jokes of those stout individuals who every evening indulged in the commonplace amusement of drinking a glass of liquor in company with girls of easy virtue.

The names of the girls on the first floor were Fernande, Raphaelle, and Rosa "the Jade." As the staff was limited, Madame had endeavored that each member of it should be a pattern, an epitome of each feminine type, so that every customer might find as nearly as possible, the realization of his ideal. Fernande represented the handsome blonde; she was very tall, rather fat, and lazy; a country girl, who could not get rid of her freckles, and whose short, light, almost colorless, tow-like hair, which was like combed-out flax, barely covered her head.

Raphaelle, who came from Marseilles, played the indispensable part of the handsome Jewess. She was thin, with high cheek-bones covered with rouge, and her black hair, which was always covered with pomatum, curled on to her forehead. Her eyes would have been handsome, if the right one had not had a speck in it. Her Roman nose came down over a square jaw, where two false upper teeth contrasted strangely with the bad color of the rest.

Rosa the Jade was a little roll of fat, nearly all stomach, with very short legs. From morning till night she sang songs, which were alternately indecent or sentimental, in a harsh voice, told silly, interminable tales, and only stopped talking in order to eat, or left off eating in order to talk. She was never still, was as active as a squirrel, in spite of her fat and her short legs; and her laugh, which was a torrent of shrill cries, resounded here and there, ceaselessly, in a bedroom, in the loft, in the *café*, everywhere, and always about nothing.

The two women on the ground floor were Louise, who was nicknamed "la Cocotte,"* and Flora, whom they called "Balancière,"† because she limped a little. The former always dressed as Liberty, with a tricolored sash, and the other as a Spanish woman, with a string of copper coins, which jingled at every step she took, in her carroty hair. Both looked like cooks dressed up for the carnival, and were like all other women of the lower orders, neither uglier nor better looking than they usually are. In fact they looked just like servants at an inn, and were generally called "the Two Pumps."

A jealous peace, very rarely disturbed, reigned among these five women, thanks to Madame's conciliatory wisdom and to her constant good humor; and the establishment, which was the only one of the kind in the little town, was very much frequented. Madame had succeeded in giving it such a respectable appearance; she was so amiable and obliging to everybody, her good heart was so well known, that she was treated with a certain amount of consideration. The regular customers spent money on her, and were delighted when she was especially friendly toward them. When they met during the day, they would say: "This evening, you know where," just as men say: "At the *café*, after dinner." In a word Madame Tellier's house was somewhere to go to, and her customers very rarely missed their daily meetings there.

One evening, toward the end of May, the first arrival, Monsieur Poulin, who was a timber merchant, and had been mayor, found the door shut. The little lantern behind the grating was not alight; there was not a sound in the house; everything seemed dead. He knocked, gently at first, and then more loudly, but nobody answered the door. Then he went slowly up the street, and when he got to the market place, he met Monsieur Duvert, the gun-maker, who was going to the same place, so they went back together, but did not meet with any better success. But suddenly they heard a loud noise close to them, and on going round the corner of the house, they saw a number of English and French sailors, who were hammering at the closed shutters of the *café* with their fists.

The two tradesmen immediately made their escape, for fear of being

* Slang for a lady of easy virtue.
† Swing, or seesaw.

compromised, but a low *Pst* stopped them; it was Monsieur Tournevau, the fish-curer, who had recognized them, and was trying to attract their attention. They told him what had happened, and he was all the more vexed at it, as he, a married man, and father of a family, only went there on Saturdays—*securitatis causa*, as he said, alluding to a measure of sanitary policy, which his friend Doctor Borde had advised him to observe. That was his regular evening, and now he would be deprived of it for the whole week.

The three men went as far as the quay together, and on the way they met young Monsieur Philippe, the banker's son, who frequented the place regularly, and Monsieur Pinipesse, the collector. They all returned to the Rue aux Juifs together, to make a last attempt. But the exasperated sailors were besieging the house, throwing stones at the shutters, and shouting, and the five first-floor customers went away as quickly as possible, and walked aimlessly about the streets.

Presently they met Monsieur Dupuis, the insurance agent, and then Monsieur Vassi, the Judge of the Tribunal of Commerce, and they all took a long walk, going to the pier first of all. There they sat down in a row on the granite parapet, and watched the rising tide, and when the promenaders had sat there for some time, Monsieur Tournevau said: "This is not very amusing!"

"Decidedly not," Monsieur Pinipesse replied, and they started off to walk again.

After going through the street on the top of the hill, they returned over the wooden bridge which crosses the Retenue, passed close to the railway, and came out again on to the market place, when suddenly a quarrel arose between Monsieur Pinipesse and Monsieur Tournevau, about an edible fungus which one of them declared he had found in the neighborhood.

As they were out of temper already from annoyance, they would very probably have come to blows, if the others had not interfered. Monsieur Pinipesse went off furious, and soon another altercation arose between the ex-mayor, Monsieur Poulin, and Monsieur Dupuis, the insurance agent, on the subject of the tax-collector's salary, and the profits which he might make. Insulting remarks were freely passing between them, when a torrent of formidable cries were heard, and the body of sailors, who were tired of waiting so long outside a closed house, came into the square. They were walking arm-in-arm, two and two, and formed a long procession, and were shouting furiously. The landsmen went and hid themselves under a gateway, and the yelling crew disappeared in the direction of the abbey. For a long time they still heard the noise, which diminished like a storm in the distance, and then silence was restored. Monsieur Poulin and Monsieur Dupuis, who were enraged with each other, went in different directions, without wishing each other good-bye.

The other four set off again, and instinctively went in the direction of

Madame Tellier's establishment, which was still closed, silent, impenetrable. A quiet, but obstinate, drunken man was knocking at the door of the *café*; then he stopped and called Frederic, the waiter, in a low voice, but finding that he got no answer, he sat down on the doorstep, and awaited the course of events.

The others were just going to retire, when the noisy band of sailors reappeared at the end of the street. The French sailors were shouting the "Marseillaise," and the Englishmen, "Rule Britannia." There was a general lurching against the wall, and then the drunken brutes went on their way toward the quay, where a fight broke out between the two nations, in the course of which an Englishman had his arm broken, and a Frenchman his nose split.

The drunken man, who had stopped outside the door, was crying by this time, as drunken men and children cry when they are vexed, and the others went away. By degrees, calm was restored in the noisy town; here and there, at moments, the distant sound of voices could be heard, only to die away in the distance.

One man was still wandering about, Monsieur Tournevau, the fish-curer, who was vexed at having to wait until the next Saturday. He hoped for something to turn up, he did not know what; but he was exasperated at the police for thus allowing an establishment of such public utility, which they had under their control, to be thus closed.

He went back to it, examined the walls, and tried to find out the reason. On the shutter he saw a notice stuck up, so he struck a wax vesta, and read the following, in a large, uneven hand: "Closed on account of the Confirmation."

Then he went away, as he saw it was useless to remain, and left the drunken man lying on the pavement fast asleep, outside the inhospitable door.

The next day, all the regular customers, one after the other, found some reason for going through the Rue aux Juifs with a bundle of papers under their arm, to keep them in countenance, and with a furtive glance they all read that mysterious notice:

"CLOSED ON ACCOUNT OF THE CONFIRMATION."

II.

Madame had a brother, who was a carpenter in their native place, Virville, in the department of Eure. When Madame had still kept the inn at Yvetot, she had stood godmother to that brother's daughter, who had received the name of Constance, Constance Rivet; she herself being a

Rivet on her father's side. The carpenter, who knew that his sister was in a good position, did not lose sight of her, although they did not meet often, as they were both kept at home by their occupations, and lived a long way from each other. But when the girl was twelve years old, and about to be confirmed, he seized the opportunity to write to his sister, and ask her to come and be present at the ceremony. Their old parents were dead, and as Madame could not well refuse, she accepted the invitation. Her brother, whose name was Joseph, hoped that by dint of showing his sister attentions, she might be induced to make her will in the girl's favor, as she had no children of her own.

His sister's occupation did not trouble his scruples in the least, and, besides, nobody knew anything about it at Virville. When they spoke of her, they only said: "Madame Tellier is living at Fécamp," which might mean that she was living on her own private income. It was quite twenty leagues from Fécamp to Virville, and for a peasant, twenty leagues on land are more than is crossing the ocean to an educated person. The people at Virville had never been further than Rouen, and nothing attracted the people from Fécamp to a village of five hundred houses, in the middle of a plain, and situated in another department. At any rate, nothing was known about her business.

But the Confirmation was coming on and Madame was in great embarrassment. She had no under-mistress, and did not at all dare to leave her house, even for a day. She feared the rivalries between the girls upstairs and those downstairs would certainly break out; that Frederic would get drunk, for when he was in that state, he would knock anybody down for a mere word. At last, however, she made up her mind to take them all with her, with the exception of the man, to whom she gave a holiday, until the next day but one.

When she asked her brother, he made no objection, but undertook to put them all up for a night. So on Saturday morning the eight o'clock express carried off Madame and her companions in a second-class carriage. As far as Beuzeille they were alone, and chattered like magpies, but at that station a couple got in. The man, an aged peasant dressed in a blue blouse with a folding collar, wide sleeves tight at the wrist, and ornamented with white embroidery, wore an old high hat with long nap. He held an enormous green umbrella in one hand, and a large basket in the other, from which the heads of three frightened ducks protruded. The woman, who sat stiffly in her rustic finery, had a face like a fowl, and with a nose that was as pointed as a bill. She sat down opposite her husband and did not stir, as she was startled at finding herself in such smart company.

There was certainly an array of striking colors in the carriage. Madame was dressed in blue silk from head to foot, and had over her dress a dazzling red shawl of imitation French cashmere. Fernande was panting in a Scottish plaid dress, whose bodice, which her companions had laced as tight as they could, had forced up her falling bosom into a double dome, that was continually heaving up and down, and which seemed liquid beneath the material. Raphaelle, with a bonnet covered with feathers, so that it looked like a nest full of birds, had on a lilac dress with gold spots on it; there was something Oriental about it that suited her Jewish face. Rosa the Jade had on a pink petticoat with large flounces, and looked like a very fat child, an obese dwarf; while the Two Pumps looked as if they had cut their dresses out of old, flowered curtains, dating from the Restoration.

Perceiving that they were no longer alone in the compartment, the ladies put on staid looks, and began to talk of subjects which might give the others a high opinion of them. But at Bolbec a gentleman with light whiskers, with a gold chain, and wearing two or three rings, got in, and put several parcels wrapped in oilcloth into the net over his head. He looked inclined for a joke, and a good-natured fellow.

"Are you ladies changing your quarters?" he asked. The question embarrassed them all considerably. Madame, however, quickly recovered her composure, and said sharply, to avenge the honor of her corps:

"I think you might try and be polite!"

He excused himself, and said: "I beg your pardon, I ought to have said your nunnery."

As Madame could not think of a retort, or perhaps as she thought herself justified sufficiently, she gave him a dignified bow, and pinched in her lips.

Then the gentleman, who was sitting between Rosa the Jade and the old peasant, began to wink knowingly at the ducks, whose heads were sticking out of the basket. When he felt that he had fixed the attention of his public, he began to tickle them under their bills, and spoke funnily to them, to make the company smile.

"We have left our little pond, qu-ack! qu-ack! to make the acquaintance of the little spit, qu-ack! qu-ack!"

The unfortunate creatures turned their necks away to avoid his caresses, and made desperate efforts to get out of their wicker prison, and then, suddenly, all at once, uttered the most lamentable quacks of distress. The women exploded with laughter. They leaned forward and pushed each other, so as to see better; they were very much interested in the ducks, and the gentleman redoubled his airs, his wit, and his teasing.

Rosa joined in, and leaning over her neighbor's legs, she kissed the three animals on the head. Immediately all the girls wanted to kiss them in turn, and the gentleman took them on to his knees, made them jump up and down and pinched them. The two peasants, who were even in greater consternation than their poultry, rolled their eyes as if they were possessed, without venturing to move, and their old wrinkled faces had not a smile nor a movement.

Then the gentleman, who was a commercial traveler, offered the ladies braces by way of a joke and taking up one of his packages, he opened it. It was a trick, for the parcel contained garters. There were blue silk, pink silk, red silk, violet silk, mauve silk garters, and the buckles were made of two gilt metal Cupids, embracing each other. The girls uttered exclamations of delight, and looked at them with that gravity which is natural to a woman when she is hankering after a bargain. They consulted one another by their looks or in a whisper, and replied in the same manner, and Madame was longingly handling a pair of orange garters that were broader and more imposing than the rest; really fit for the mistress of such an establishment.

"Come, my kittens," he said, "you must try them on."

There was a torrent of exclamations, and they squeezed their petticoats between their legs, as if they thought he was going to ravish them, but he quietly waited his time, and said: "Well, if you will not, I shall pack them up again."

And he added cunningly: "I offer any pair they like, to those who will try them on."

But they would not, and sat up very straight, and looked dignified.

But the Two Pumps looked so distressed that he renewed the offer to them. Flora especially hesitated, and he pressed her:

"Come, my dear, a little courage! Just look at that lilac pair; it will suit your dress admirably."

That decided her, and pulling up her dress she showed a thick leg fit for a milk-maid, in a badly-fitting, coarse stocking. The commercial traveler stooped down and fastened the garter below the knee first of all and then above it; and he tickled the girl gently, which made her scream and jump. When he had done, he gave her the lilac pair, and asked: "Who next?"

"I! I!" they all shouted at once, and he began on Rosa the Jade, who uncovered a shapeless, round thing without any ankle, a regular "sausage of a leg," as Raphaelle used to say.

The commercial traveler complimented Fernande, and grew quite enthusiastic over her powerful columns.

The thin tibias of the handsome Jewess met with less flattery, and Louise Cocotte, by way of a joke, put her petticoats over the man's head, so that Madame was obliged to interfere to check such unseemly behavior.

Lastly, Madame herself put out her leg, a handsome, muscular, Norman leg, and in his surprise and pleasure the commercial traveler gallantly took off his hat to salute that master calf, like a true French cavalier.

The two peasants, who were speechless from surprise, looked askance, out of the corners of their eyes. They looked so exactly like fowls, that the man with the light whiskers, when he sat up, said "Co—co—ri—co," under their very noses, and that gave rise to another storm of amusement.

The old people got out at Motteville, with their basket, their ducks, and their umbrella, and they heard the woman say to her husband, as they went away:

"They are sluts, who are off to that cursed place, Paris."

The funny commercial traveler himself got out at Rouen, after behaving so coarsely that Madame was obliged sharply to put him into his right place. She added, as a moral: "This will teach us not to talk to the first comer."

At Oissel they changed trains, and at a little station further on Monsieur Joseph Rivet was waiting for them with a large cart and a number of chairs in it, which was drawn by a white horse.

The carpenter politely kissed all the ladies, and then helped them into his conveyance.

Three of them sat on three chairs at the back, Raphaelle, Madame, and her brother on the three chairs in front, and Rosa, who had no seat, settled herself as comfortably as she could on tall Fernande's knees, and then they set off.

But the horse's jerky trot shook the cart so terribly, that the chairs began to dance, throwing the travelers into the air, to the right and to the left, as if they had been dancing puppets. This made them make horrible grimaces and screams, which, however, were cut short by another jolt of the cart.

They clung to the sides of the vehicle, their bonnets fell on to their backs, their noses on their shoulders, and the white horse trotted on, stretching out his head and holding out his tail quite straight, a little hairless rat's tail, with which he whisked his buttocks from time to time.

Joseph Rivet, with one leg on the shafts and the other bent under him, held the reins with elbows high and kept uttering a kind of chuckling sound, which made the horse prick up its ears and go faster.

The green country extended on either side of the road, and here and there the colza in flower presented a waving expanse of yellow, from which there arose a strong, wholesome, sweet and penetrating smell, which the wind carried to some distance.

The cornflowers showed their little blue heads among the rye, and the women wanted to pick them, but Monsieur Rivet refused to stop.

Then sometimes a whole field appeared to be covered with blood, so thickly were the poppies growing, and the car, which looked as if it were filled with flowers of more brilliant hue, drove on through the fields colored with wild flowers, to disappear behind the trees of a farm, then to reappear and go on again through the yellow or green standing crops studded with red or blue.

One o'clock struck as they drove up to the carpenter's door. They were tired out, and very hungry, as they had eaten nothing since they left home. Madame Rivet ran out, and made them alight, one after another, kissing them as soon as they were on the ground. She seemed as if she would never tire of kissing her sister-in-law, whom she apparently wanted to monopolize. They had lunch in the workshop, which had been cleared out for the next day's dinner.

A capital omelette, followed by boiled chitterlings, and washed down by good, sharp cider, made them all feel comfortable.

Rivet had taken a glass so that he might hob-nob with them, and his wife cooked, waited on them, brought in the dishes, took them out, and asked all of them in a whisper whether they had everything they wanted. A number of boards standing against the walls, and heaps of shavings that had been swept into the corners, gave out the smell of planed wood, of carpentering, that resinous odor which penetrates the lungs.

They wanted to see the little girl, but she had gone to church, and would not be back until evening, so they all went out for a stroll in the country.

It was a small village, through which the high road passed. Ten or a dozen houses on either side of the single street had for tenants the butcher, the grocer, the carpenter, the innkeeper, the shoe-maker, and the baker, and others.

The church was at the end of the street. It was surrounded by a small churchyard, and four enormous lime-trees, which stood just outside the porch, shaded it completely. It was built of flint, in no particular style, and had a slated steeple. When you got past it, you were in the open country again, which was broken here and there by clumps of trees which hid some homestead.

Rivet had given his arm to his sister, out of politeness, although he was in his working clothes, and was walking with her majestically. His wife, who was overwhelmed by Raphaelle's gold-striped dress, was walking between her and Fernande, and rotund Rosa was trotting behind with Louise Cocotte and Flora, the seesaw, who was limping along, quite tired out.

The inhabitants came to their doors, the children left off playing, and a window curtain would be raised, so as to show a muslin cap, while an old woman with a crutch, who was almost blind, crossed herself as if it were a religious procession. They all looked for a long time after those handsome ladies from the town, who had come so far to be present at the confirmation of Joseph Rivet's little girl, and the carpenter rose very much in the public estimation.

As they passed the church, they heard some children singing; little shrill voices were singing a hymn, but Madame would not let them go in, for fear of disturbing the little cherubs.

After a walk, during which Joseph Rivet enumerated the principal landed proprietors, spoke about the yield of the land, and the productiveness of the cows and sheep, he took his flock of women home and installed them in his house, and as it was very small, he had put them into the rooms, two and two.

Just for once, Rivet would sleep in the workshop on the shavings; his wife was going to share her bed with her sister-in-law, and Fernande and Raphaelle were to sleep together in the next room. Louise and Flora were put into the kitchen, where they had a mattress on the floor, and Rosa had a little dark cupboard at the top of the stairs to herself, close to the loft, where the candidate for confirmation was to sleep.

When the girl came in, she was overwhelmed with kisses; all the women wished to caress her, with that need of tender expansion, that habit of professional wheedling, which had made them kiss the ducks in the railway carriage.

They took her on to their laps, stroked her soft, light hair, and pressed her in their arms with vehement and spontaneous outbursts of affection, and the child, who was very good-natured and docile, bore it all patiently.

As the day had been a fatiguing one for everybody, they all went to bed soon after dinner. The whole village was wrapped in that perfect stillness of the country, which is almost like a religious silence, and the girls who were accustomed to the noisy evenings of their establishment, felt rather impressed by the perfect repose of the sleeping village. They shivered, not with cold, but with those little shivers of solitude which come over uneasy and troubled hearts.

As soon as they were in bed, two and two together, they clasped each other in their arms, as if to protect themselves against this feeling of the calm and profound slumber of the earth. But Rosa the Jade, who was alone in her little dark cupboard, felt a vague and painful emotion come over her.

She was tossing about in bed, unable to get to sleep, when she heard the faint sobs of a crying child close to her head, through the partition. She was frightened, and called out, and was answered by a weak voice, broken by sobs. It was the little girl who, being used to sleeping in her mother's room, was frightened in her small attic.

Rosa was delighted, got up softly so as not to awaken anyone, and went and fetched the child. She took her into her warm bed, kissed her and pressed her to her bosom, caressed her, lavished exaggerated manifestations of tenderness on her, and at last grew calmer herself and went to sleep. And till morning, the candidate for confirmation slept with her head on Rosa's naked bosom.

At five o'clock, the little church bell ringing the "Angelus" woke these women up, who as a rule slept the whole morning long.

The peasants were up already, and the women went busily from house to house, carefully bringing short, starched, muslin dresses in bandboxes, or very long wax tapers, with a bow of silk fringed with gold in the middle, and with dents in the wax for the fingers.

The sun was already high in the blue sky, which still had a rosy tint toward the horizon, like a faint trace of dawn, remaining. Families of fowls were walking about the henhouses, and here and there a black cock, with a glistening breast, raised his head, crowned by his red comb, flapped his wings, and uttered his shrill crow, which the other cocks repeated.

Vehicles of all sorts came from neighboring parishes, and discharged tall, Norman women, in dark dresses, with neck-handkerchiefs crossed over the bosom, and fastened with silver brooches, a hundred years old.

The men had put on blouses over their new frock coats, or over their old dress coats of green cloth, the tails of which hung down below their blouses. When the horses were in the stable, there was a double line of rustic conveyances along the road; carts, cabriolets, tilburies, char-à-bancs, traps of every shape and age, resting on their shafts, or pointing them in the air.

The carpenter's house was as busy as a beehive. The ladies, in dressing jackets and petticoats, with their long, thin, light hair, which looked as if it were faded and worn by dyeing, were busy dressing the child, who was standing motionless on a table, while Madame Tellier was directing the movements of her battalion. They washed her, did her hair, dressed her, and with the help of a number of pins, they arranged the folds of her dress, and took in the waist, which was too large.

Then, when she was ready, she was told to sit down and not to move, and the women hurried off to get ready themselves.

The church bell began to ring again, and its tinkle was lost in the air, like a feeble voice which is soon drowned in space. The candidates came out of the houses, and went toward the parochial building which contained the school and the mansion house. This stood quite at one end of the village, while the church was situated at the other.

The parents, in their very best clothes, followed their children with awkward looks, and with the clumsy movements of bodies that are always bent at work.

The little girls disappeared in a cloud of muslin, which looked like whipped cream, while the lads, who looked like embryo waiters in a *café*, and whose heads shone with pomatum, walked with their legs apart, so as not to get any dust or dirt on to their black trousers.

It was something for the family to be proud of; a large number of relatives from distant parts surrounded the child, and, consequently, the carpenter's triumph was complete.

Madame Tellier's regiment, with its mistress at its head, followed Constance; her father gave his arm to his sister, her mother walked by the side of Raphaelle, Fernande with Rosa, and the Two Pumps together. Thus they walked majestically through the village, like a general's staff in full uniform, while the effect on the village was startling.

At the school, the girls arranged themselves under the Sister of Mercy, and the boys under the schoolmaster, and they started off, singing a hymn as they went. The boys led the way, in two files, between the two rows of vehicles, from which the horses had been taken out, and the girls followed in the same order. As all the people in the village had given the town ladies the precedence out of politeness, they came immediately behind the girls, and lengthened the double line of the procession still more, three on the right and three on the left, while their dresses were as striking as a bouquet of fireworks.

When they went into the church, the congregation grew quite excited. They pressed against each other, they turned round, they jostled one another in order to see. Some of the devout ones almost spoke aloud, so astonished were they at the sight of these ladies, whose dresses were trimmed more elaborately than the priest's chasuble.

The Mayor offered them his pew, the first one on the right, close to the choir, and Madame Tellier sat there with her sister-in-law; Fernande and Raphaelle, Rosa the Jade, and the Two Pumps occupied the second seat, in company with the carpenter.

The choir was full of kneeling children, the girls on one side, and the boys on the other, and the long wax tapers which they held looked like lances, pointing in all directions. Three men were standing in front of the lectern, singing as loud as they could.

They prolonged the syllables of the sonorous Latin indefinitely, holding on to the Amens with interminable *a—a's*, which the serpent of the organ kept up in the monotonous, long-drawn-out notes, emitted by the deep-throated pipes.

A child's shrill voice took up the reply, and from time to time a priest sitting in a stall and wearing a biretta, got up, muttered something, and sat down again. The three singers continued, with their eyes fixed on the big book of plain-song lying open before them on the outstretched wings of an eagle, mounted on a pivot.

Then silence ensued. The service went on, and toward the end of it, Rosa, with her head in both her hands, suddenly thought of her mother, and her village church on a similar occasion. She almost fancied that that day had returned, when she was so small, and almost hidden in her white dress, and she began to cry.

First of all she wept silently, the tears dropped slowly from her eyes, but her emotion increased with her recollections, and she began to sob. She took out her pocket-handkerchief, wiped her eyes, and held it to her mouth, so as not to scream, but it was useless.

A sort of rattle escaped her throat, and she was answered by two other profound, heart-breaking sobs; for her two neighbors, Louise and Flora, who were kneeling near her, overcome by similar recollections, were sobbing by her side. There was a flood of tears, and as weeping is contagious, Madame soon found that her eyes were wet, and on turning to her sister-in-law, she saw that all the occupants of the pew were crying.

Soon, throughout the church, here and there, a wife, a mother, a sister, seized by the strange sympathy of poignant emotion, and agitated by the grief of those handsome ladies on their knees, who were shaken by their sobs, was moistening her cambric pocket-handkerchief, and pressing her beating heart with her left hand.

Just as the sparks from an engine will set fire to dry grass, so the tears of Rosa and of her companions infected the whole congregation in a moment. Men, women, old men, and lads in new blouses were soon sobbing; something superhuman seemed to be hovering over their heads—a spirit, the powerful breath of an invisible and all-powerful being.

Suddenly a species of madness seemed to pervade the church, the noise of a crowd in a state of frenzy, a tempest of sobs and of stifled cries. It passed over the people like gusts of wind which bow the trees in a forest, and the priest, overcome by emotion, stammered out incoherent prayers, those inarticulate prayers of the soul, when it soars toward heaven.

The people behind him gradually grew calmer. The cantors, in all the dignity of their white surplices, went on in somewhat uncertain voices, and the organ itself seemed hoarse, as if the instrument had been weeping. The priest, however, raised his hand, as a sign for them to be still, and went to the chancel steps. All were silent, immediately.

After a few remarks on what had just taken place, which he attributed to a miracle, he continued, turning to the seats where the carpenter's guests were sitting:

"I especially thank you, my dear sisters, who have come from such a distance, and whose presence among us, whose evident faith and ardent piety have set such a salutary example to all. You have edified my parish; your emotion has warmed all hearts; without you, this day would not, perhaps, have had this really divine character. It is sufficient, at times, that there should be one chosen to keep in the flock, to make the whole flock blessed."

His voice failed him again, from emotion, and he said no more, but concluded the service.

They all left the church as quickly as possible; the children themselves were restless, tired with such a prolonged tension of the mind. Besides, the elders were hungry, and one after another left the churchyard, to see about dinner.

There was a crowd outside, a noisy crowd, a babel of loud voices, in which the shrill Norman accent was discernible. The villagers formed two ranks, and when the children appeared, each family seized their own.

The whole houseful of women caught hold of Constance, surrounded her and kissed her, and Rosa was especially demonstrative. At last she took hold of one hand, while Madame Tellier held the other, and Raphaelle and Fernande held up her long muslin petticoat, so that it might not drag in the dust. Louise and Flora brought up the rear with Madame Rivet, and the child, who was very silent and thoughtful, set off home, in the midst of this guard of honor.

The dinner was served in the workshop, on long boards supported by trestles, and through the open door they could see all the enjoyment that was going on. Everywhere people were feasting; through every window could be seen tables surrounded by people in their Sunday clothes. There was merriment in every house—men sitting in their shirt sleeves, drinking cider, glass after glass.

In the carpenter's house the gaiety took on somewhat of an air of reserve, the consequence of the emotion of the girls in the morning. Rivet was the only one who was in good cue, and he was drinking to excess. Madame Tellier was looking at the clock every moment, for, in order not to lose two days following, they ought to take the 3.55 train, which would bring them to Fécamp by dark.

The carpenter tried very hard to distract her attention, so as to keep his guests until the next day. But he did not succeed, for she never joked when there was business to be done, and as soon as they had had their coffee she ordered her girls to make haste and get ready. Then, turning to her brother, she said:

"You must have the horse put in immediately," and she herself went to complete her preparations.

When she came down again, her sister-in-law was waiting to speak to her about the child, and a long conversation took place, in which, however, nothing was settled. The carpenter's wife finessed, and pretended to be very much moved, and Madame Tellier, who was holding the girl on her knees, would not pledge herself to anything definite, but merely gave vague promises: she would not forget her, there was plenty of time, and then, they were sure to meet again.

But the conveyance did not come to the door, and the women did not come downstairs. Upstairs, they even heard loud laughter, falls, little screams, and much clapping of hands, and so, while the carpenter's wife went to the stable to see whether the cart was ready, Madame went upstairs.

Rivet, who was very drunk and half undressed, was vainly trying to kiss Rosa, who was choking with laughter. The Two Pumps were holding him by the arms and trying to calm him, as they were shocked at such a scene after that morning's ceremony; but Raphaelle and Fernande were urging him on, writhing and holding their sides with laughter, and they uttered shrill cries at every useless attempt that the drunken fellow made.

The man was furious, his face was red, his dress disordered, and he was trying to shake off the two women who were clinging to him, while he was pulling Rosa's bodice, with all his might, and ejaculating: "Won't you, you slut?"

But Madame, who was very indignant, went up to her brother, seized him by the shoulders, and threw him out of the room with such violence that he fell against a wall in the passage, and a minute afterward, they heard him pumping water on to his head in the yard. When he came back with the cart, he was already quite calmed down.

They seated themselves in the same way as they had done the day before, and the little white horse started off with his quick, dancing trot. Under the hot sun, their fun, which had been checked during dinner, broke out again. The girls now were amused at the jolts which the wagon gave, pushed their neighbors' chairs, and burst out laughing every moment, for they were in the vein for it, after Rivet's vain attempt.

There was a haze over the country, the roads were glaring, and dazzled their eyes. The wheels raised up two trails of dust, which followed the cart for a long time along the high road, and presently Fernande, who was fond of music, asked Rosa to sing something. She boldly struck up the "Gros Curé de Meudon," but Madame made her stop immediately as she thought it a song which was very unsuitable for such a day, and added:

"Sing us something of Béranger's."

After a moment's hesitation, Rosa began Béranger's song, "The Grandmother," in her worn-out voice, and all the girls, and even Madame herself, joined in the chorus:

> "How I regret
> My dimpled arms,
> My well-made legs,
> And my vanished charms!"

"That is first-rate," Rivet declared, carried away by the rhythm. They shouted the refrain to every verse, while Rivet beat time on the shafts with his foot, and on the horse's back with the reins. The animal, himself, carried away by the rhythm, broke into a wild gallop, and threw all the women in a heap, one on top of the other, in the bottom of the conveyance.

They got up, laughing as if they were crazy, and the song went on, shouted at the top of their voices, beneath the burning sky and among the ripening grain, to the rapid gallop of the little horse, who set off every time the refrain was sung, and galloped a hundred yards, to their great delight. Occasionally a stone breaker by the roadside sat up, and looked at the wild and shouting female load, through his wire spectacles.

When they got out at the station, the carpenter said:

"I am sorry you are going; we might have had some fun together."

But Madame replied very sensibly: "Everything has its right time, and we cannot always be enjoying ourselves."

And then he had a sudden inspiration: "Look here, I will come and see you at Fécamp next month." And he gave a knowing look, with his bright and roguish eyes.

"Come," Madame said, "you must be sensible; you may come if you like, but you are not to be up to any of your tricks."

He did not reply, and as they heard the whistle of the train he immediately began to kiss them all. When it came to Rosa's turn, he tried to get to her mouth, which she, however, smiling with her lips closed, turned away from him each time by a rapid movement of her head to one side. He held her in his arms, but he could not attain his object, as his large whip, which he was holding in his hand and waving behind the girl's back in desperation, interfered with his efforts.

"Passengers for Rouen, take your seats, please!" a guard cried, and they got in. There was a slight whistle followed by a loud one from the engine, which noisily puffed out its first jet of steam, while the wheels began to turn a little, with visible effort. Rivet left the station and went to the gate by the side of the line to get another look at Rosa, and as the carriage full of human merchandise passed him, he began to crack his whip and to jump, singing at the top of his voice:

> "How I regret
> My dimpled arms,
> My well-made legs,
> And my vanished charms!"

And then he watched a white pocket-handkerchief, which somebody was waving, as it disappeared in the distance.

III.

They slept the peaceful sleep of quiet consciences, until they got to Rouen. When they returned to the house, refreshed and rested, Madame could not help saying:

"It was all very well, but I was already longing to get home."

They hurried over their supper, and then, when they had put on their usual light evening costumes, waited for their usual customers. The little colored lamp outside the door told the passers-by that the flock had returned to the fold, and in a moment the news spread, nobody knew how, or by whom.

Monsieur Philippe, the banker's son, even carried his audacity so far as to send a special messenger to Monsieur Tournevau who was in the bosom of his family.

The fish-curer used every Sunday to have several cousins to dinner, and they were having coffee, when a man came in with a letter in his hand. Monsieur Tournevau was much excited; he opened the envelope and grew pale; it only contained these words in pencil:

"The cargo of fish has been found; the ship has come into port; good business for you. Come immediately."

He felt in his pockets, gave the messenger two-pence, and suddenly blushing to his ears, he said: "I must go out." He handed his wife the laconic and mysterious note, rang the bell, and when the servant came in, he asked her to bring him his hat and overcoat immediately. As soon as he was in the street, he began to run, and the way seemed to him to be twice as long as usual, in consequence of his impatience.

Madame Tellier's establishment had put on quite a holiday look. On the ground floor, a number of sailors were making a deafening noise, and Louise and Flora drank with one and the other, so as to merit their name of the Two Pumps more than ever. They were being called for everywhere at once; already they were not quite sober enough for their business, and the night bid fair to be a very jolly one.

The upstairs room was full by nine o'clock. Monsieur Vassi, the Judge of the Tribunal of Commerce, Madame's usual Platonic wooer, was talking to her in a corner, in a low voice, and they were both smiling, as if they were about to come to an understanding.

Monsieur Poulin, the ex-mayor, was holding Rosa on his knees; and she, with her nose close to his, was running her hands through the old gentleman's white whiskers.

Tall Fernande, who was lying on the sofa, had both her feet on Monsieur Pinipesse the tax-collector's stomach, and her back on young Monsieur Philippe's waistcoat; her right arm was round his neck, and she held a cigarette in her left.

Raphaelle appeared to be discussing matters with Monsieur Dupuis, the insurance agent, and she finished by saying: "Yes, my dear, I will."

Just then, the door opened suddenly, and Monsieur Tournevau came in. He was greeted with enthusiastic cries of: "Long live Tournevau!" and

Raphaelle, who was twirling round, went and threw herself into his arms. He seized her in a vigorous embrace, and without saying a word, lifting her up as if she had been a feather, he carried her through the room.

Rosa was chatting to the ex-mayor, kissing him every moment, and pulling both his whiskers at the same time in order to keep his head straight.

Fernande and Madame remained with the four men, and Monsieur Philippe exclaimed: "I will pay for some champagne; get three bottles, Madame Tellier." And Fernande gave him a hug, and whispered to him: "Play us a waltz, will you?" So he rose and sat down at the old piano in the corner, and managed to get a hoarse waltz out of the entrails of the instrument.

The tall girl put her arms round the tax-collector, Madame asked Monsieur Vassi to take her in his arms, and the two couples turned round, kissing as they danced. Monsieur Vassi, who had formerly danced in good society, waltzed with such elegance that Madame was quite captivated.

Frederic brought the champagne; the first cork popped, and Monsieur Philippe played the introduction to a quadrille, through which the four dancers walked in society fashion, decorously, with propriety of deportment, with bows, and curtsies, and then they began to drink.

Monsieur Philippe next struck up a lively polka, and Monsieur Tournevau started off with the handsome Jewess, whom he held up in the air, without letting her feet touch the ground. Monsieur Pinipesse and Monsieur Vassi had started off with renewed vigor and from time to time one or other couple would stop to toss off a long glass of sparkling wine. The dance was threatening to become never-ending, when Rosa opened the door.

"I want to dance," she exclaimed. And she caught hold of Monsieur Dupuis, who was sitting idle on the couch, and the dance began again.

But the bottles were empty. "I will pay for one," Monsieur Tournevau said.

"So will I," Monsieur Vassi declared.

"And I will do the same," Monsieur Dupuis remarked.

They all began to clap their hands, and it soon became a regular ball. From time to time, Louise and Flora ran upstairs quickly, had a few turns while their customers downstairs grew impatient, and then they returned regretfully to the *café*. At midnight they were still dancing.

Madame shut her eyes to what was going on, and she had long private talks in corners with Monsieur Vassi, as if to settle the last details of something that had already been agreed upon.

At last, at one o'clock, the two married men, Monsieur Tournevau and Monsieur Pinipesse, declared that they were going home, and wanted to pay. Nothing was charged for except the champagne, and that only cost six francs a bottle, instead of ten, which was the usual price, and when they expressed their surprise at such generosity, Madame, who was beaming, said to them:

"We don't have a holiday every day."

Mademoiselle Fifi

THE MAJOR GRAF* von Farlsberg, the Prussian commandant, was reading his newspaper, lying back in a great armchair, with his booted feet on the beautiful marble fireplace, where his spurs had made two holes, which grew deeper every day, during the three months that he had been in the château of Urville.

A cup of coffee was smoking on a small, inlaid table, which was stained with liquors, burnt by cigars, notched by the penknife of the victorious officer, who occasionally would stop while sharpening a pencil, to jot down figures, or to make a drawing on it, just as it took his fancy.

When he had read his letters and the German newspapers, which his baggage-master had brought him, he got up, and after throwing three or four enormous pieces of green wood on to the fire—for these gentlemen were gradually cutting down the park in order to keep themselves warm—he went to the window. The rain was descending in torrents, a regular Normandy rain, which looked as if it were being poured out by some furious hand, a slanting rain, which was as thick as a curtain, and which formed a kind of wall with oblique stripes, and which deluged everything, a regular rain, such as one frequently experiences in the neighborhood of Rouen, which is the watering-pot of France.

For a long time the officer looked at the sodden turf, and at the swollen Andelle beyond it, which was overflowing its banks, and he was drumming a waltz from the Rhine on the windowpanes, with his fingers, when a noise made him turn round; it was his second in command, Captain Baron von Kelweinstein.

The major was a giant, with broad shoulders, and a long, fair beard,

* Count.

which hung like a cloth on to his chest. His whole, solemn person suggested the idea of a military peacock, a peacock who was carrying his tail spread out on to his breast. He had cold, gentle, blue eyes, and the scar from a sword-cut, which he had received in the war with Austria; he was said to be an honorable man, as well as a brave officer.

The captain, a short, red-faced man, who was tightly girthed in at the waist, had his red hair cropped quite close to his head, and in certain lights almost looked as if he had been rubbed over with phosphorus. He had lost two front teeth one night, though he could not quite remember how. This defect made him speak so that he could not always be understood, and he had a bald patch on the top of his head, which made him look rather like a monk, with a fringe of curly, bright, golden hair round the circle of bare skin.

The commandant shook hands with him, and drank his cup of coffee (the sixth that morning) at a draught, while he listened to his subordinate's report of what had occurred; and then they both went to the window, and declared that it was a very unpleasant outlook. The major, who was a quiet man, with a wife at home, could accommodate himself to everything; but the captain, who was rather fast, being in the habit of frequenting low resorts, and much given to women, was mad at having been shut up for three months in the compulsory chastity of that wretched hole.

There was a knock at the door, and when the commandant said, "Come in," one of their automatic soldiers appeared, and by his mere presence announced that breakfast was ready. In the dining-room, they met three other officers of lower rank: a lieutenant, Otto von Grossling, and two sub-lieutenants, Fritz Scheunebarg, and Count von Eyrick, a very short, fair-haired man, who was proud and brutal toward men, harsh toward prisoners, and very violent.

Since he had been in France, his comrades had called him nothing but "Mademoiselle Fifi." They had given him that nickname on account of his dandified style and small waist, which looked as if he wore stays, from his pale face, on which his budding mustache scarcely showed, and on account of the habit he had acquired of employing the French expression, *fi, fi donc,* which he pronounced with a slight whistle, when he wished to express his sovereign contempt for persons or things.

The dining-room of the château was a magnificent long room, whose fine old mirrors, now cracked by pistol bullets, and Flemish tapestry, now cut to ribbons and hanging in rags in places, from sword-cuts, told too well what Mademoiselle Fifi's occupation was during his spare time.

There were three family portraits on the walls; a steel-clad knight, a cardinal, and a judge, who were all smoking long porcelain pipes, which had been inserted into holes in the canvas, while a lady in a long, pointed waist proudly exhibited an enormous pair of mustaches, drawn with a piece of charcoal.

The officers ate their breakfast almost in silence in that mutilated room, which looked dull in the rain, and melancholy under its vanquished appearance, although its old, oak floor had become as solid as the stone floor of a public-house.

When they had finished eating, and were smoking and drinking, they began, as usual, to talk about the dull life they were leading. The bottles of brandy and of liquors passed from hand to hand, and all sat back in their chairs, taking repeated sips from their glasses, and scarcely removing the long, bent stems, which terminated in china bowls painted in a manner to delight a Hottentot, from their mouths.

As soon as their glasses were empty, they filled them again, with a gesture of resigned weariness, but Mademoiselle Fifi emptied his every minute, and a soldier immediately gave him another. They were enveloped in a cloud of strong tobacco smoke; they seemed to be sunk in a state of drowsy, stupid intoxication, in that dull state of drunkenness of men who have nothing to do, when suddenly, the baron sat up, and said: "By heavens! This cannot go on; we must think of something to do." And on hearing this, Lieutenant Otto and Sub-lieutenant Fritz, who preeminently possessed the grave, heavy German countenance, said: "What, Captain?"

He thought for a few moments, and then replied: "What? Well, we must get up some entertainment, if the commandant will allow us."

"What sort of an entertainment, captain?" the major asked, taking his pipe out of his mouth.

"I will arrange all that, commandant," the baron said: "I will send *Le Devoir* to Rouen, who will bring us some ladies. I know where they can be found. We will have supper here, as all the materials are at hand, and, at least, we shall have a jolly evening."

Graf von Farlsberg shrugged his shoulders with a smile: "You must surely be mad, my friend."

But all the other officers got up, surrounded their chief, and said: "Let captain have his own way, commandant; it is terribly dull here."

And the major ended by yielding. "Very well," he replied, and the baron immediately sent for *Le Devoir*.

The latter was an old corporal who had never been seen to smile, but who carried out all orders of his superiors to the letter, no matter what they might be. He stood there, with an impassive face, while he received the baron's instructions, and then went out; five minutes later a large wagon belonging to the military train, covered with a miller's tilt, galloped off as fast as four horses could take it, under the pouring rain, and the officers all seemed to awaken from their lethargy, their looks brightened, and they began to talk.

Although it was raining as hard as ever, the major declared that it was not so dull, and Lieutenant von Grossling said with conviction, that the sky was clearing up, while Mademoiselle Fifi did not seem to be able to keep in his place. He got up, and sat down again, and his bright eyes seemed to be looking for something to destroy. Suddenly, looking at the lady with the mustaches, the young fellow pulled out his revolver, and said: "You shall not see it." And without leaving his seat he aimed, and with two successive bullets cut out both the eyes of the portrait.

"Let us make a mine!" he then exclaimed, and the conversation was suddenly interrupted, as if they had found some fresh and powerful subject of interest. The mine was his invention, his method of destruction, and his favorite amusement.

When he left the château, the lawful owner, Count Fernand d'Amoys d'Urville, had not had time to carry away or to hide anything, except the plate, which had been stowed away in a hole made in one of the walls, so that, as he was very rich and had good taste, the large drawing-room, which opened into the dining-room, had looked like the gallery in a museum, before his precipitate flight.

Expensive oil-paintings, water-colors, and drawings hung upon the walls, while on the tables, on the hanging shelves, and in elegant glass cupboards, there were a thousand knickknacks: small vases, statuettes, groups in Dresden china, grotesque Chinese figures, old ivory, and Venetian glass, which filled the large room with their precious and fantastical array.

Scarcely anything was left now; not that the things had been stolen, for the major would not have allowed that, but Mademoiselle Fifi *would have a mine*, and on that occasion all the officers thoroughly enjoyed themselves for five minutes. The little marquis went into the drawing-room to get what he wanted, and he brought back a small, delicate china teapot, which he filled with gun-powder, and carefully introduced a piece of German tinder into it, through the spout. Then he lighted it, and took this infernal machine in to the next room; but he came back immediately, and shut the door. The Germans all stood expectantly, their faces full of childish, smiling curiosity, and as soon as the explosion had shaken the château, they all rushed in at once.

Mademoiselle Fifi, who got in first, clapped his hands in delight at the sight of a terra-cotta Venus, whose head had been blown off, and each picked up pieces of porcelain, and wondered at the strange shape of the fragments, while the major was looking with a paternal eye at the large drawing-room which had been wrecked in such a Neronic fashion, and which was strewn with the fragments of works of art. He went out first, and said, with a smile: "He managed that very well!"

But there was such a cloud of smoke in the dining-room mingled with the tobacco smoke, that they could not breathe, so the commandant opened the window, and all the officers, who had gone into the room for a glass of cognac, went up to it.

The moist air blew into the room, and brought a sort of spray with it, which powdered their beards. They looked at the tall trees which were dripping with the rain, at the broad valley which was covered with mist, and at the church spire in the distance, which rose up like a gray point in the beating rain.

The bells had not rung since their arrival. That was the only resistance which the invaders had met with in the neighborhood. The parish priest had not refused to take in and to feed the Prussian soldiers; he had several times even drunk a bottle of beer or claret with the hostile commandant, who often employed him as a benevolent intermediary; but it was no use to ask him for a single stroke of the bells; he would sooner have allowed himself to be shot. That was his way of protesting against the invasion, a peaceful and silent protest, the only one, he said, which was suitable to a priest, who was a man of mildness, and not of blood; and everyone, for twenty-five miles round, praised Abbé Chantavoine's firmness and heroism, in venturing to proclaim the public mourning by the obstinate silence of his church bells.

The whole village grew enthusiastic over his resistance, and was ready to back up their pastor and to risk anything, as they looked upon that silent protest as the safeguard of the national honor. It seemed to the peasants that thus they had deserved better of their country than Belfort and Strassburg, that they had set an equally valuable example, and that the name of their little village would become immortalized by that; but with that exception, they refused their Prussian conquerors nothing.

The commandant and his officers laughed among themselves at that inoffensive courage, and as the people in the whole country round showed themselves obliging and compliant toward them, they willingly tolerated their silent patriotism. Only little Count Wilhelm would have liked to have forced them to ring the bells. He was very angry at his superior's politic compliance with the priest's scruples, and every day he begged the commandant to allow him to sound "ding-dong, ding-dong," just once, only just once, just by way of a joke. And he asked it like a wheedling woman, in the tender voice of some mistress who wishes to obtain something, but the commandant would not yield, and to console *herself*, Mademoiselle Fifi made a *mine* in the château.

The five men stood there together for some minutes, inhaling the moist air, and at last, Lieutenant Fritz said, with a laugh: "The ladies will certainly not have fine weather for their drive." Then they separated, each to his own duties, while the captain had plenty to do in seeing about the dinner.

When they met again, as it was growing dark, they began to laugh at seeing each other as dandified and smart as on the day of a grand review. The commandant's hair did not look as gray as it did in the morning, and the captain had shaved—had only kept his mustache on, which made him look as if he had a streak of fire under his nose.

In spite of the rain, they left the window open, and one of them went to listen from time to time. At a quarter past six the baron said he heard a rumbling in the distance. They all rushed down, and soon the wagon drove up at a gallop with its four horses, splashed up to their backs, steaming and panting. Five women got out at the bottom of the steps, five handsome girls whom a comrade of the captain, to whom *Le Devoir* had taken his card, had selected with care.

They had not required much pressing, as they were sure of being well treated, for they had got to know the Prussians in the three months during which they had had to do with them. So they resigned themselves to the men as they did to the state of affairs. "It is part of our business, so it must be done," they said as they drove along; no doubt to allay some slight, secret scruples of conscience.

They went into the dining-room immediately, which looked still more dismal in its dilapidated state, when it was lighted up; while the table covered with choice dishes, the beautiful china and glass, and the plate, which had been found in the hole in the wall where its owner had hidden it, gave to the place the look of a bandits' resort, where they were supping after committing a robbery. The captain was radiant; he took hold of the women as if he were familiar with them; appraising them, kissing them, valuing them for what they were worth as *ladies of pleasure*; and when the three young men wanted to appropriate one each, he opposed them authoritatively, reserving to himself the right to apportion them justly, according to their several ranks, so as not to wound the hierarchy. There-fore, so as to avoid all discussion, jarring, and suspicion of partiality, he placed them all in a line according to height, and addressing the tallest, he said in a voice of command:

"What is your name?"

"Pamela," she replied, raising her voice.

Then he said: "Number One, called Pamela, is adjudged to the com-mandant."

Then, having kissed Blondina, the second, as a sign of proprietorship, he proffered stout Amanda to Lieutenant Otto, Eva, "the Tomato," to Sub-lieutenant Fritz, and Rachel, the shortest of them all, a very young, dark girl, with eyes as black as ink, a Jewess, whose snub nose confirmed by exception the rule which allots hooked noses to all her race, to the youngest officer, frail Count Wilhelm von Eyrick.

They were all pretty and plump, without any distinctive features, and all were very much alike in look and person, from their daily dissipation, and the life common to houses of public accommodation.

The three younger men wished to carry off their women immediately, under the pretext of finding them brushes and soap; but the captain wisely opposed this, for he said they were quite fit to sit down to dinner, and that those who went up would wish for a change when they came down, and so would disturb the other couples, and his experience in such matters carried the day. There were only many kisses; expectant kisses.

Suddenly Rachel choked, and began to cough until the tears came into her eyes, while smoke came through her nostrils. Under pretense of kissing her, the count had blown a whiff of tobacco into her mouth. She did not fly into a rage, and did not say a word, but she looked at her possessor with latent hatred in her dark eyes.

They sat down to dinner. The commandant seemed delighted; he made Pamela sit on his right, and Blondina on his left, and said, as he unfolded his table napkin: "That was a delightful idea of yours, captain."

Lieutenants Otto and Fritz, who were as polite as if they had been with fashionable ladies, rather intimidated their neighbors, but Baron von Kelweinstein gave the reins to all his vicious propensities, beamed, made doubtful remarks, and seemed on fire with his crown of red hair. He paid them compliments in French from the other side of the Rhine, and sputtered out gallant remarks, only fit for a low pothouse, from between his two broken teeth.

They did not understand him, however, and their intelligence did not seem to be awakened until he uttered nasty words and broad expressions, which were mangled by his accent. Then all began to laugh at once, like mad women, and fell against each other, repeating the words, which the baron then began to say all wrong, in order that he might have the pleasure of hearing them say doubtful things. They gave him as much of that stuff as he wanted, for they were drunk after the first bottle of wine, and, becoming themselves once more, and opening the door to their usual habits, they kissed the mustaches on the right and left of them, pinched their arms, uttered furious cries, drank out of every glass, and sang French couplets, and bits of German songs, which they had picked up in their daily intercourse with the enemy.

Soon the men themselves, intoxicated by that which was displayed to their sight and touch, grew very amorous, shouted and broke the plates and dishes, while the soldiers behind them waited on them stolidly. The commandant was the only one who put any restraint upon himself.

Mademoiselle Fifi had taken Rachel on to his knees, and, getting excited, at one moment kissed the little black curls on her neck, inhaling the pleasant warmth of her body, and all the savor of her person, through the slight space there was between her dress and her skin, and at another pinched her furiously through the material, and made her scream, for he was seized with a species of ferocity, and tormented by his desire to hurt her. He often held her close to him, as if to make her part of himself, and put his lips in a long kiss on the Jewess's rosy mouth, until she lost her breath; and at last he bit her until a stream of blood ran down her chin and on to her bodice.

For the second time, she looked him full in the face, and as she bathed the wound, she said: "You will have to pay for that!"

But he merely laughed a hard laugh, and said: "I will pay."

At dessert, champagne was served, and the commandant rose, and in the same voice in which he would have drunk to the health of the Empress Augusta, he drank: "To our ladies!" Then a series of toasts began, toasts worthy of the lowest soldiers and of drunkards, mingled with filthy jokes, which were made still more brutal by their ignorance of the language. They got up, one after the other, trying to say something witty, forcing themselves to be funny, and the women, who were so drunk that they almost fell off their chairs, with vacant looks and clammy tongues, applauded madly each time.

The captain, who no doubt wished to impart an appearance of gallantry to the orgy, raised his glass again, and said: "To our victories over hearts!" Thereupon Lieutenant Otto, who was a species of bear from the Black Forest, jumped up, inflamed and saturated with drink, and seized by an access of alcoholic patriotism, cried: "To our victories over France!"

Drunk as they were, the women were silent, and Rachel turned round with a shudder, and said: "Look here, I know some Frenchmen, in whose presence you would not dare to say that." But the little count, still holding her on his knees, began to laugh, for the wine had made him very merry, and said: "Ha! ha! ha! I have never met any of them, myself. As soon as we show ourselves, they run away!"

The girl, who was in a terrible rage, shouted into his face: "You are lying, you dirty scoundrel!"

For a moment, he looked at her steadily, with his bright eyes upon her, as he had looked at the portrait before he destroyed it with revolver bullets, and then he began to laugh: "Ah! yes, talk about them, my dear! Should we be here now, if they were brave?" Then getting excited, he exclaimed: "We are the masters! France belongs to us!" She jumped off his knees with a bound, and threw herself into her chair, while he rose, held out his glass over the table, and repeated: "France and the French, the woods, the fields, and the houses of France belong to us!"

The others, who were quite drunk, and who were suddenly seized by military enthusiasm, the enthusiasm of brutes, seized their glasses, and shouting, "Long live Prussia!" emptied them at a draught.

The girls did not protest, for they were reduced to silence, and were afraid. Even Rachel did not say a word, as she had no reply to make, and then the little count put his champagne glass, which had just been refilled, on to the head of the Jewess, and exclaimed: "All the women in France belong to us, also!"

At that she got up so quickly that the glass upset, spilling the amber colored wine on to her black hair as if to baptize her, and broke into a hundred fragments as it fell on to the floor. With trembling lips, she defied the looks of the officer, who was still laughing, and she stammered out, in a voice choked with rage: "That—that—that—is not true,—for you shall certainly not have any French women."

He sat down again, so as to laugh at his ease, and trying effectually to speak in the Parisian accent, he said: "That is good, very good! Then what did you come here for, my dear?"

She was thunderstruck, and made no reply for a moment, for in her agitation she did not understand him at first; but as soon as she grasped his meaning, she said to him indignantly and vehemently: "I! I! am not a woman; I am only a strumpet, and that is all that Prussians want."

Almost before she had finished, he slapped her full in her face; but as he was raising his hand again, as if he would strike her, she, almost mad with passion, took up a small dessert knife from the table, and stabbed him right in the neck, just above the breastbone. Something that he was going to say, was cut short in his throat, and he sat there, with his mouth half open, and a terrible look in his eyes.

All the officers shouted in horror, and leaped up tumultuously; but throwing her chair between Lieutenant Otto's legs, who fell down at full length, she ran to the window, opened it before they could seize her, and jumped out into the night and pouring rain.

In two minutes, Mademoiselle Fifi was dead. Fritz and Otto drew their swords and wanted to kill the women, who threw themselves at their feet and clung to their knees. With some difficulty the major stopped the slaughter, and had the four terrified girls locked up in a room under the care of two soldiers. Then he organized the pursuit of the fugitive, as carefully as if he were about to engage in a skirmish, feeling quite sure that she would be caught.

The table, which had been cleared immediately, now served as a bed on which to lay Fifi out, and the four officers made for the window, rigid and sobered, with the stern faces of soldiers on duty, and tried to pierce through the darkness of the night, amid the steady torrent of rain. Suddenly, a shot was heard, and then another, a long way off; and for four hours they heard, from time to time, near or distant reports and rallying cries, strange words uttered as a call, in guttural voices.

In the morning they all returned. Two soldiers had been killed and three others wounded by their comrades in the ardor of that chase, and in the confusion of such a nocturnal pursuit, but they had not caught Rachel.

Then the inhabitants of the district were terrorized, the houses were turned topsy-turvy, the country was scoured and beaten up, over and over again, but the Jewess did not seem to have left a single trace of her passage behind her.

When the general was told of it, he gave orders to hush up the affair, so as not to set a bad example to the army, but he severely censured the commandant, who in turn punished his inferiors. The general had said: "One does not go to war in order to amuse oneself, and to caress prostitutes." And Graf von Farlsberg, in his exasperation, made up his mind to have his revenge on the district, but as he required a pretext for showing severity, he sent for the priest, and ordered him to have the bell tolled at the funeral of Count von Eyrick.

Contrary to all expectation, the priest showed himself humble and most respectful, and when Mademoiselle Fifi's body left the Château d'Urville on its way to the cemetery, carried by soldiers, preceded, surrounded, and followed by soldiers, who marched with loaded rifles, for the first time the bell sounded its funereal knell in a lively manner, as if a friendly hand were caressing it. At night it sounded again, and the next day, and every day; it rang as much as anyone could desire. Sometimes even, it would start at night, and sound gently through the darkness, seized by strange joy, awakened, one could not tell why. All the peasants in the neighborhood declared that it was bewitched, and nobody, except the priest and the sacristan would now go near the church tower, and they went because a poor girl was living there in grief and solitude, secretly nourished by those two men.

She remained there until the German troops departed, and then one evening the priest borrowed the baker's cart, and himself drove his prisoner to Rouen. When they got there, he embraced her, and she quickly went back on foot to the establishment from which she had come, where the proprietress, who thought that she was dead, was very glad to see her.

A short time afterward, a patriot who had no prejudices, who liked her because of her bold deed, and who afterward loved her for herself, married her, and made a lady of her.

Miss Harriet

THERE WERE SEVEN of us in a four-in-hand, four women and three men, one of whom was on the box seat beside the coachman. We were following, at a foot pace, the broad highway which serpentines along the coast.

Setting out from Etretat at break of day, in order to visit the ruins of Tancarville, we were still asleep, chilled by the fresh air of the morning. The women, especially, who were but little accustomed to these early excursions, let their eyelids fall and rise every moment, nodding their heads or yawning, quite insensible to the glory of the dawn.

It was autumn. On both sides of the road the bare fields stretched out, yellowed by the corn and wheat stubble which covered the soil like a bristling growth of beard. The spongy earth seemed to smoke. Larks were singing high up in the air, while other birds piped in the bushes.

At length the sun rose in front of us, a bright red on the plane of the horizon; and as it ascended, growing clearer from minute to minute, the country seemed to awake, to smile, to shake and stretch itself, like a young girl who is leaving her bed in her white airy chemise. The Count d'Etraille, who was seated on the box, cried:

"Look! look! a hare!" and he pointed toward the left, indicating a piece of hedge. The leveret threaded its way along, almost concealed by the field, only its large ears visible. Then it swerved across a deep rut, stopped, again pursued its easy course, changed its direction, stopped anew, disturbed, spying out every danger, and undecided as to the route it should take. Suddenly it began to run, with great bounds from its hind legs, disappearing finally in a large patch of beet-root. All the men had woke up to watch the course of the beast.

René Lemanoir then exclaimed:

"We are not at all gallant this morning," and looking at his neighbor, the little Baroness of Stérennes, who was struggling with drowsiness, he said to her in a subdued voice: "You are thinking of your husband, Baroness. Reassure yourself; he will not return before Saturday, so you have still four days."

She responded to him with a sleepy smile:

"How rude you are." Then, shaking off her torpor, she added: "Now, let somebody say something that will make us all laugh. You, Monsieur

Chenal, who have the reputation of possessing a larger fortune than the Duke of Richelieu, tell us a love story in which you have been mixed up, anything you like."

Léon Chenal, an old painter, who had once been very handsome, very strong, who was very proud of his physique and very amiable, took his long white beard in his hand and smiled; then, after a few moments' reflection, he became suddenly grave.

"Ladies, it will not be an amusing tale; for I am going to relate to you the most lamentable love affair of my life, and I sincerely hope that none of my friends has ever passed through a similar experience.

I.

"At that time I was twenty-five years old, and was making daubs along the coast of Normandy. I call 'making daubs' that wandering about, with a bag on one's back, from mountain to mountain, under the pretext of studying and of sketching nature. I know nothing more enjoyable than that happy-go-lucky wandering life, in which you are perfectly free, without shackles of any kind, without care, without pre-occupation, without thought even of to-morrow. You go in any direction you please, without any guide save your fancy, without any counselor save your eyes. You pull up, because a running brook seduces you, or because you are attracted, in front of an inn, by the smell of potatoes frying. Sometimes it is the perfume of clematis which decides you in your choice, or the naïve glance of the servant at an inn. Do not despise me for my affection for these rustics. These girls have soul as well as feeling, not to mention firm cheeks and fresh lips; while their hearty and willing kisses have the flavor of wild fruit. Love always has its price, come whence it may. A heart that beats when you make your appearance, an eye that weeps when you go away, these are things so rare, so sweet, so precious, that they must never be despised.

"I have had rendezvous in ditches in which cattle repose, and in barns among the straw, still steaming from the heat of the day. I have recollections of canvas spread on rude and creaky benches, and of hearty, fresh, free kisses, more delicate, free from affectation, and sincere than the subtle attractions of charming and distinguished women.

"But what you love most amid all these varied adventures are the country, the woods, the risings of the sun, the twilight, the light of the moon. For the painter these are honeymoon trips with Nature. You are alone with her in that long and tranquil rendezvous. You go to bed in the fields amid marguerites and wild poppies, and, with eyes wide open, you watch the going down of the sun, and descry in the distance the little village, with its pointed clock-tower, which sounds the hour of midnight.

"You sit down by the side of a spring which gushes out from the foot of an oak, amid a covering of fragile herbs, growing and redolent of life. You go down on your knees, bend forward, and drink the cold and pellucid water, wetting your mustache and nose; you drink it with a physical pleasure, as though you were kissing the spring, lip to lip. Sometimes, when you encounter a deep hole, along the course of these tiny brooks, you plunge into it, quite naked, and on your skin, from head to foot, like an icy and delicious caress, you feel the lovely and gentle quivering of the current.

"You are gay on the hills, melancholy on the verge of pools, exalted when the sun is crowned in an ocean of blood-red shadows, and when it casts on the rivers its red reflection. And at night, under the moon, as it passes the vault of heaven, you think of things, singular things, which would never have occurred to your mind under the brilliant light of day.

"So, in wandering through the same country we are in this year, I came to the little village of Benouville, on the Falaise, between Yport and Etretat. I came from Fécamp, following the coast, a high coast, perpendicular as a wall, with projecting and rugged rocks falling sheer down into the sea. I had walked since the morning on the close clipped grass, as smooth and as yielding as a carpet. Singing lustily, I walked with long strides, looking sometimes at the slow and lazy flight of a gull, with its short, white wings, sailing in the blue heavens, sometimes at the green sea, or at the brown sails of a fishing bark. In short, I had passed a happy day, a day of listlessness and of liberty.

"I was shown a little farmhouse, where travelers were put up, a kind of inn, kept by a peasant, which stood in the center of a Norman court, surrounded by a double row of beeches.

"Quitting the Falaise, I gained the hamlet, which was hemmed in by trees, and I presented myself at the house of Mother Lecacheur.

"She was an old, wrinkled, and austere rustic, who always seemed to yield to the pressure of new customs with a kind of contempt.

"It was the month of May: the spreading apple-trees covered the court with a whirling shower of blossoms which rained unceasingly both upon people and upon the grass.

"I said:

" 'Well, Madame Lecacheur, have you a room for me?'

"Astonished to find that I knew her name, she answered:

" 'That depends; everything is let; but, all the same, there will be no harm in looking.'

"In five minutes we were in perfect accord, and I deposited my bag upon the bare floor of a rustic room, furnished with a bed, two chairs, a table, and a washstand. The room opened into the large and smoky kitchen, where the lodgers took their meals with the people of the farm and with the farmer himself, who was a widower.

"I washed my hands, after which I went out. The old woman was fricasseeing a chicken for dinner in a large fireplace, in which hung the stew-pot, black with smoke.

" 'You have travelers, then, at the present time?' said I to her.

"She answered in an offended tone of voice:

" 'I have a lady, an English lady, who has attained to years of maturity. She is occupying my other room.'

"By means of an extra five sous a day, I obtained the privilege of dining out in the court when the weather was fine.

"My cover was then placed in front of the door, and I commenced to gnaw with hunger the lean members of the Normandy chicken, to drink the clear cider, and to munch the hunk of white bread, which, though four days old, was excellent.

"Suddenly, the wooden barrier which opened on to the highway was opened, and a strange person directed her steps toward the house. She was very slender, very tall, enveloped in a Scotch shawl with red borders. You would have believed that she had no arms, if you had not seen a long hand appear just above the hips, holding a white tourist umbrella. The face of a mummy, surrounded with sausage rolls of plaited gray hair, which bounded at every step she took, made me think, I know not why, of a sour herring adorned with curling papers. Lowering her eyes, she passed quickly in front of me, and entered the house.

"This singular apparition made me curious. She undoubtedly was my neighbor, the aged English lady of whom our hostess had spoken.

"I did not see her again that day. The next day, when I had begun to paint at the end of that beautiful valley, which you know extends as far as Etretat, lifting my eyes suddenly, I perceived something singularly attired standing on the crest of the declivity; it looked like a pole decked out with flags. It was she. On seeing me, she suddenly disappeared. I re-entered the house at midday for lunch, and took my seat at the common table, so as to make the acquaintance of this old and original creature. But she did not respond to my polite advances, was insensible even to my little attentions. I poured water out for her with great alacrity, I passed her the dishes with great eagerness. A slight, almost imperceptible movement of the head, and an English word, murmured so low that I did not understand it, were her only acknowledgments.

"I ceased occupying myself with her, although she had disturbed my thoughts. At the end of three days, I knew as much about her as did Madame Lecacheur herself.

"She was called Miss Harriet. Seeking out a secluded village in which to pass the summer, she had been attracted to Benouville, some six months before, and did not seem disposed to quit it. She never spoke at table, ate rapidly, reading all the while a small book, treating of some Protestant propaganda. She gave a copy of it to everybody. The curé himself had received no less than four copies, at the hands of an urchin to whom she had paid two sous' commission. She said sometimes to our hostess, abruptly, without preparing her in the least for the declaration:

" 'I love the Saviour more than all; I worship him in all creation; I adore him in all nature; I carry him always in my heart.'

"And she would immediately present the old woman with one of her brochures which were destined to convert the universe.

"In the village she was not liked. In fact, the schoolmaster had declared that she was an atheist, and that a sort of reproach attached to her. The curé, who had been consulted by Madame Lecacheur, responded:

" 'She is a heretic, but God does not wish the death of the sinner, and I believe her to be a person of pure morals.'

"These words, 'atheist,' 'heretic,' words which no one can precisely define, threw doubts into some minds. It was asserted, however, that this English-woman was rich, and that she had passed her life in traveling through every country in the world, because her family had thrown her off. Why had her family thrown her off? Because of her natural impiety?

"She was, in fact, one of those people of exalted principles, one of those opinionated puritans of whom England produces so many, one of those good and insupportable old women who haunt the *tables d'hôte* of every hotel in Europe, who spoil Italy, poison Switzerland, render the charming cities of the Mediterranean uninhabitable, carry everywhere their fantastic manias, their petrified vestal manners, their indescribable toilettes, and a certain odor of india-rubber, which makes one believe that at night they slip themselves into a case of that material. When I meet one of these people in a hotel, I act like birds which see a manikin in a field.

"This woman, however, appeared so singular that she did not displease me.

"Madame Lecacheur, hostile by instinct to everything that was not rustic, felt in her narrow soul a kind of hatred for the ecstatic extravagances of the old girl. She had found a phrase by which to describe her, I know not how, but a phrase assuredly contemptuous, which had sprung to her lips, invented probably by some confused and mysterious travail of soul. She said: 'That woman is a demoniac.' This phrase as uttered by that austere and sentimental creature, seemed to me irresistibly comic. I, myself, never called her now anything else but 'the demoniac,' feeling a singular pleasure in pronouncing this word on seeing her.

"I would ask Mother Lecacheur: 'Well, what is our demoniac about to-day?' To which my rustic friend would respond, with an air of having been scandalized:

" 'What do you think, sir? She has picked up a toad which has had its leg battered, and carried it to her room, and has put it in her washstand, and dressed it up like a man. If that is not profanation, I should like to know what is!'

"On another occasion, when walking along the Falaise, she had bought a large fish which had just been caught, simply to throw it back into the sea again. The sailor, from whom she had bought it, though paid handsomely, was greatly provoked at this act—more exasperated, indeed, than if she had put her hand into his pocket and taken his money. For a whole month he could not speak of the circumstance without getting into a fury and denouncing it as an outrage. Oh yes! She was indeed a demoniac, this Miss Harriet, and Mother Lecacheur must have had an inspiration of genius in thus christening her.

"The stable-boy, who was called Sapeur, because he had served in Africa in his youth, entertained other aversions. He said, with a roguish air: 'She is an old hag who has lived her days.' If the poor woman had but known!

"Little kind-hearted Céleste did not wait upon her willingly, but I was never able to understand why. Probably her only reason was that she was a stranger, of another race, of a different tongue, and of another religion. She was in good truth a demoniac!

"She passed her time wandering about the country, adoring and searching for God in nature. I found her one evening on her knees in a cluster of bushes. Having discovered something red through the leaves, I brushed aside the branches, and Miss Harriet at once rose to her feet, confused at having been found thus, looking at me with eyes as terrible as those of a wild cat surprised in open day.

"Sometimes, when I was working among the rocks, I would suddenly descry her on the banks of the Falaise standing like a semaphore signal. She gazed passionately at the vast sea, glittering in the sunlight, and the boundless sky empurpled with fire. Sometimes I would distinguish her at the bottom of an alley, walking quickly, with her elastic English step; and I would go toward her, attracted by I know not what, simply to see her illuminated visage, her dried-up features, which seemed to glow with an ineffable, inward, and profound happiness.

"Often I would encounter her in the corner of a field sitting on the grass, under the shadow of an apple-tree, with her little Bible lying open on her knee, while she looked meditatively into the distance.

"I could no longer tear myself away from that quiet country neighborhood, bound to it as I was by a thousand links of love for its soft and sweeping landscapes. At this farm I was out of the world, far removed from everything, but in close proximity to the soil, the good, healthy, beautiful green soil. And, must I avow it, there was something besides curiosity which retained me at the residence of Mother Lecacheur. I wished to become acquainted a little with this strange Miss Harriet, and to learn what passes in the solitary souls of those wandering old, English dames.

II.

"We became acquainted in a rather singular manner. I had just finished a study which appeared to me to display genius and power; as it must have, since it was sold for ten thousand francs, fifteen years later. It was as simple, however, as that two and two make four, and had nothing to do with academic rules. The whole of the right side of my canvas represented a rock, an enormous rock, covered with sea-wrack, brown, yellow, and red, across which the sun poured like a stream of oil. The light, without which one could see the stars concealed in the background, fell upon the stone, and gilded it as if with fire. That was all. A first stupid attempt at dealing with light, with burning rays, with the sublime.

"On the left was the sea, not the blue sea, the slate-colored sea, but a sea of jade, as greenish, milky, and thick as the overcast sky.

"I was so pleased with my work that I danced from sheer delight as I carried it back to the inn. I wished that the whole world could have seen it at one and the same moment. I can remember that I showed it to a cow which was browsing by the wayside, exclaiming, at the same time: 'Look at that, my old beauty; you will not often see its like again.'

"When I had reached the front of the house, I immediately called out to Mother Lecacheur, shouting with all my might:

" 'Ohé! Ohé! my mistress, come here and look at this.'

"The rustic advanced and looked at my work with stupid eyes, which distinguished nothing, and did not even recognize whether the picture was the representation of an ox or a house.

"Miss Harriet came into the house, and passed in rear of me just at the moment when, holding out my canvas at arm's length, I was exhibiting it to the female innkeeper. The 'demoniac' could not help but see it, for I took care to exhibit the thing in such a way that it could not escape her notice. She stopped abruptly and stood motionless, stupefied. It was her rock which was depicted, the one which she usually climbed to dream away her time undisturbed.

"She uttered a British 'Oh,' which was at once so accentuated and so flattering, that I turned round to her smiling, and said:

" 'This is my latest work, Mademoiselle.'

"She murmured ecstatically, comically, and tenderly:

" 'Oh! Monsieur, you must understand what it is to have a palpitation.'

"I colored up, of course, and was more excited by that compliment than if it had come from a queen. I was seduced, conquered, vanquished. I could have embraced her—upon my honor.

"I took my seat at the table beside her, as I had always done. For the first time, she spoke, drawling out in a loud voice:

" 'Oh! I love nature so much.'

"I offered her some bread, some water, some wine. She now accepted these with the vacant smile of a mummy. I began to converse with her about the scenery.

"After the meal, we rose from the table together and walked leisurely across the court; then, attracted by the fiery glow which the setting sun cast over the surface of the sea, I opened the outside gate which faced in the direction of the Falaise, and we walked on side by side, as satisfied as any two persons could be who have just learned to understand and penetrate each other's motives and feelings.

"It was a misty, relaxing evening, one of those enjoyable evenings which impart happiness to mind and body alike. All is joy, all is charm. The luscious and balmy air, loaded with the perfumes of herbs, with the perfumes of grass-wrack, with the odor of the wild flowers, caresses the soul with a penetrating sweetness. We were going to the brink of the abyss which overlooked the vast sea and rolled past us at the distance of less than a hundred meters.

"We drank with open mouth and expanded chest, that fresh breeze from the ocean which glides slowly over the skin, salted as it is by long contact with the waves.

"Wrapped up in her square shawl, inspired by the balmy air and with teeth firmly set, the English-woman gazed fixedly at the great sun-ball, as it descended toward the sea. Soon its rim touched the waters, just in rear of a ship which had appeared on the horizon, until, by degrees, it was swallowed up by the ocean. We watched it plunge, diminish, and finally disappear.

"Miss Harriet contemplated with passionate regard the last glimmer of the flaming orb of day.

"She muttered: 'Oh! love—I love—' I saw a tear start in her eye. She continued: 'I wish I were a little bird, so that I could mount up into the firmament.'

"She remained standing as I had often before seen her, perched on the river bank, her face as red as her flaming shawl. I should have liked to have sketched her in my album. It would have been an ecstatic caricature. I turned my face away from her so as to be able to laugh.

"I then spoke to her of painting, as I would have done to a fellow-artist, using the technical terms common among the devotees of the profession. She listened attentively to me, eagerly seeking to divine the sense of the obscure words, so as to penetrate my thoughts. From time to time, she would exclaim: 'Oh! I understand, I understand. This is very interesting.' We returned home.

"The next day, on seeing me, she approached me eagerly, holding out her hand; and we became firm friends immediately.

"She was a brave creature, with an elastic sort of a soul, which became enthusiastic at a bound. She lacked equilibrium, like all women who are spinsters at the age of fifty. She seemed to be pickled in vinegary innocence, though her heart still retained something of youth and of girlish effervescence. She loved both nature and animals with a fervent ardor, a love like old wine, mellow through age, with a sensual love that she had never bestowed on men.

"One thing is certain: a mare roaming in a meadow with a foal at its side, a bird's nest full of young ones, squeaking, with their open mouths and enormous heads, made her quiver with the most violent emotion.

"Poor solitary beings! Sad wanderers from *table d'hôte* to *table d'hôte*, poor beings, ridiculous and lamentable, I love you ever since I became acquainted with Miss Harriet!

"I soon discovered that she had something she would like to tell me, but dared not, and I was amused at her timidity. When I started out in the morning with my box on my back, she would accompany me as far as the end of the village, silent, but evidently struggling inwardly to find words with which to begin a conversation. Then she would leave me abruptly, and, with jaunty step, walk away quickly.

"One day, however, she plucked up courage:

" 'I would like to see how you paint pictures? Will you show me? I have been very curious.'

"And she colored up as though she had given utterance to words extremely audacious.

"I conducted her to the bottom of the Petit-Val, where I had commenced a large picture.

"She remained standing near me, following all my gestures with concentrated attention. Then, suddenly, fearing, perhaps, that she was disturbing me, she said to me: 'Thank you,' and walked away.

"But in a short time she became more familiar, and accompanied me every day, her countenance exhibiting visible pleasure. She carried her folding stool under her arm, would not consent to my carrying it, and she sat always by my side. She would remain there for hours immovable and mute, following with her eye the point of my brush in its every movement.

When I would obtain, by a large splatch of color spread on with a knife, a striking and unexpected effect, she would, in spite of herself, give vent to a half-suppressed 'Oh!' of astonishment, of joy, of admiration. She had the most tender respect for my canvases, an almost religious respect for that human reproduction of a part of nature's work divine. My studies appeared to her to be pictures of sanctity, and sometimes she spoke to me of God, with the idea of converting me.

"Oh! He was a queer good-natured being, this God of hers. He was a sort of village philosopher without any great resources, and without great power; for she always figured him to herself as a being quivering over injustices committed under his eyes, and helpless to prevent them.

"She was, however, on excellent terms with him, affecting even to be the confidant of his secrets and of his whims. She said:

" 'God wills, or God does not will,' just like a sergeant announcing to a recruit: 'The colonel has commanded.'

"At the bottom of her heart she deplored my ignorance of the intention of the Eternal, which she strove, nay, felt herself compelled, to impart to me.

"Almost every day, I found in my pockets, in my hat when I lifted it from the ground, in my box of colors, in my polished shoes, standing in the mornings in front of my door, those little pious brochures, which she, no doubt, received directly from Paradise.

"I treated her as one would an old friend, with unaffected cordiality. But I soon perceived that she had changed somewhat in her manner; but, for a while, I paid little attention to it.

"When I walked about, whether to the bottom of the valley, or through some country lanes, I would see her suddenly appear, as though she were returning from a rapid walk. She would then sit down abruptly, out of breath, as though she had been running or overcome by some profound emotion. Her face would be red, that English red which is denied to the people of all other countries; then, without any reason, she would grow pale, become the color of the ground, and seem ready to faint away. Gradually, however, I would see her regain her ordinary color, whereupon she would begin to speak.

"Then, without warning, she would break off in the middle of a sentence, spring up from her seat, and march off so rapidly and so strongly, that it would, sometimes, put me to my wits' end to try and discover whether I had done or said anything to displease or offend her.

"I finally came to the conclusion that this arose from her early habits and training, somewhat modified, no doubt, in honor of me, since the first days of our acquaintanceship.

"When she returned to the farm, after walking for hours on the wind-beaten coast, her long curled hair would be shaken out and hanging loose, as though it had broken away from its bearings. It was seldom that this gave her any concern; though sometimes she looked as though she had been dining *sans cérémonie;* her locks having become disheveled by the breezes.

"She would then go up to her room in order to adjust what I called her glass lamps. When I would say to her, in familiar gallantry, which, however, always offended her:

" 'You are as beautiful as a planet to-day, Miss Harriet,' a little blood would immediately mount into her cheeks, the blood of a young maiden, the blood of sweet fifteen.

"Then she would become abruptly savage and cease coming to watch me paint. But I always thought:

" 'This is only a fit of temper she is passing through.'

"But it did not always pass away. When I spoke to her sometimes, she would answer me, either with an air of affected indifference, or in sullen anger; and she became by turns rude, impatient, and nervous. For a time I never saw her except at meals, and we spoke but little. I concluded, at length, that I must have offended her in something; and, accordingly, I said to her one evening:

" 'Miss Harriet, why is it that you do not act toward me as formerly? What have I done to displease you? You are causing me much pain!'

"She responded, in an angry tone, in a manner altogether *sui generis:*

" 'I am always with you the same as formerly. It is not true, not true,' and she ran upstairs and shut herself up in her room.

"At times she would look upon me with strange eyes. Since that time I have often said to myself that those condemned to death must look thus when informed that their last day has come. In her eye there lurked a species of folly, a folly at once mysterious and violent—even more, a fever, an exasperated desire, impatient, at once incapable of being realized and unrealizable!

"Nay, it seemed to me that there was also going on within her a combat, in which her heart struggled against an unknown force that she wished to overcome—perhaps, even, something else. But what could I know? What could I know?

III

"This was indeed a singular revelation.

"For some time I had commenced to work, as soon as daylight appeared, on a picture, the subject of which was as follows:

"A deep ravine, steep banks dominated by two declivities, lined with brambles and long rows of trees, hidden, drowned in milky vapor, clad in that misty robe which sometimes floats over valleys at break of day. At the extreme end of that thick and transparent fog, you see coming, or rather already come, a human couple, a stripling and a maiden embraced, interlaced, she, with head leaning on him, he, inclined toward her, and lip to lip.

"A ray of the sun, glistening through the branches, has traversed the fog of dawn and illuminated it with a rosy reflection, just behind the rustic lovers, whose vague shadows are reflected on it in clear silver. It was well done, yes, indeed, well done.

"I was working on the declivity which led to the Val d'Etretat. This particular morning, I had, by chance, the sort of floating vapor which was necessary for my purpose. Suddenly, an object appeared in front of me, a kind of phantom; it was Miss Harriet. On seeing me, she took to flight. But I called after her saying: 'Come here, come here, Mademoiselle, I have a nice little picture for you.'

"She came forward, though with seeming reluctance. I handed her my sketch. She said nothing, but stood for a long time motionless, looking at it. Suddenly she burst into tears. She wept spasmodically, like men who have been struggling hard against shedding tears, but who can do so no longer, and abandon themselves to grief, though unwillingly. I got up, trembling, moved myself by the sight of a sorrow I did not comprehend, and I took her by the hand with a gesture of brusque affection, a true French impulse which impels one quicker than one thinks.

"She let her hands rest in mine for a few seconds and I felt them quiver, as if her whole nervous system was twisting and turning. Then she withdrew her hands abruptly, or, rather, tore them out of mine.

"I recognized that shiver as soon as I had felt it; I was deceived in nothing. Ah! the love shudder of a woman, whether she is fifteen or fifty years of age, whether she is one of the people or one of the *monde*, goes so straight to my heart that I never had any difficulty in understanding it!

"Her whole frail being trembled, vibrated, yielded. I knew it. She walked away before I had time to say a word, leaving me as surprised as if I had witnessed a miracle, and as troubled as if I had committed a crime.

"I did not go in to breakfast. I took a walk on the banks of the Falaise, feeling that I could just as soon weep as laugh, looking on the adventure as both comic and deplorable, and my position as ridiculous, fain to believe that I had lost my head.

"I asked myself what I ought to do. I debated whether I ought not to take my leave of the place and almost immediately my resolution was formed.

"Somewhat sad and perplexed, I wandered about until dinner time, and entered the farmhouse just when the soup had been served up.

"I sat down at the table, as usual. Miss Harriet was there, munching away solemnly, without speaking to anyone, without even lifting her eyes. She wore, however, her usual expression, both of countenance and manner.

"I waited, patiently, till the meal had been finished. Then, turning toward the landlady, I said: 'Madame Lecacheur, it will not be long now before I shall have to take my leave of you.'

"The good woman, at once surprised and troubled, replied in a quivering voice: 'My dear sir, what is it I have just heard you say? Are you going to leave us, after I have become so much accustomed to you?'

"I looked at Miss Harriet from the corner of my eye. Her countenance did not change in the least; but the under-servant came toward me with eyes wide open. She was a fat girl, of about eighteen years of age, rosy, fresh, strong as a horse, yet possessing a rare attribute in one in her position—she was very neat and clean. I had kissed her at odd times, in out of the way corners, in the manner of a mountain guide, nothing more.

"The dinner being over, I went to smoke my pipe under the apple-trees, walking up and down at my ease, from one end of the court to the other. All the reflections which I had made during the day, the strange discovery of the morning, that grotesque and passionate attachment for me, the recollections which that revelation had suddenly called up, recollections at once charming and perplexing, perhaps, also, that look which the servant had cast on me at the announcement of my departure—all these things, mixed up and combined, put me now in an excited bodily state, with the tickling sensation of kisses on my lips, and in my veins something which urged me on to commit some folly.

"Night having come on, casting its dark shadows under the trees, I descried Céleste, who had gone to shut the hen-coops, at the other end of the inclosure. I darted toward her, running so noiselessly that she heard nothing, and as she got up from closing the small traps by which the chickens went in and out, I clasped her in my arms and rained on her coarse, fat face a shower of kisses. She made a struggle, laughing all the same, as she was accustomed to do in such circumstances. What made me suddenly loose my grip of her? Why did I at once experience a shock? What was it that I heard behind me?

"It was Miss Harriet who had come upon us, who had seen us, and who stood in front of us, as motionless as a specter. Then she disappeared in the darkness.

"I was ashamed, embarrassed, more annoyed at having been surprised by her than if she had caught me committing some criminal act.

"I slept badly that night; I was worried and haunted by sad thoughts. I seemed to hear loud weeping; but in this I was no doubt deceived.

Moreover, I thought several times that I heard some one walking up and down in the house, and that some one opened my door from the outside.

"Toward morning, I was overcome by fatigue, and sleep seized on me. I got up late and did not go downstairs until breakfast time, being still in a bewildered state, not knowing what kind of face to put on.

"No one had seen Miss Harriet. We waited for her at table, but she did not appear. At length, Mother Lecacheur went to her room. The Englishwoman had gone out. She must have set out at break of day, as she was wont to do, in order to see the sun rise.

"Nobody seemed astonished at this and we began to eat in silence.

"The weather was hot, very hot, one of those still sultry days when not a leaf stirs. The table had been placed out of doors, under an apple-tree; and from time to time Sapeur had gone to the cellar to draw a jug of cider, everybody was so thirsty. Céleste brought the dishes from the kitchen, a ragout of mutton with potatoes, a cold rabbit, and a salad. Afterward she placed before us a dish of strawberries, the first of the season.

"As I wanted to wash and freshen these, I begged the servant to go and bring a pitcher of cold water.

"In about five minutes she returned, declaring that the well was dry. She had lowered the pitcher to the full extent of the cord, and had touched the bottom, but on drawing the pitcher up again, it was empty. Mother Lecacheur, anxious to examine the thing for herself, went and looked down the hole. She returned announcing that one could see clearly something in the well, something altogether unusual. But this, no doubt, was pottles of straw, which, out of spite, had been cast down it by a neighbor.

"I wished also to look down the well, hoping to clear up the mystery, and perched myself close to its brink. I perceived, indistinctly, a white object. What could it be? I then conceived the idea of lowering a lantern at the end of a cord. When I did so, the yellow flame danced on the layers of stone and gradually became clearer. All four of us were leaning over the opening, Sapeur and Céleste having now joined us. The lantern rested on a black and white, indistinct mass, singular, incomprehensible. Sapeur exclaimed:

" 'It is a horse. I see the hoofs. It must have escaped from the meadow, during the night, and fallen in headlong.'

"But, suddenly, a cold shiver attacked my spine. I first recognized a foot, then a clothed limb; the body was entire, but the other limb had disappeared under the water.

"I groaned and trembled so violently that the light of the lamp danced hither and thither over the object, discovering a slipper.

" 'It is a woman! who—who—can it be? It is Miss Harriet.'

"Sapeur alone did not manifest horror. He had witnessed many such scenes in Africa.

"Mother Lecacheur and Céleste began to scream and to shriek, and ran away.

"But it was necessary to recover the corpse of the dead. I attached the boy securely by the loins to the end of the pulley-rope; then I lowered him slowly, and watched him disappear in the darkness. In the one hand he had a lantern, and held on to the rope with the other. Soon I recognized his voice, which seemed to come from the center of the earth, crying:

" 'Stop.'

"I then saw him fish something out of the water. It was the other limb. He bound the two feet together, and shouted anew:

" 'Haul up.'

"I commenced to wind him up, but I felt my arms strain, my muscles twitch, and was in terror lest I should let the boy fall to the bottom. When his head appeared over the brink, I asked:

" 'What is it?' as though I only expected that he would tell me what he had discovered at the bottom.

"We both got on to the stone slab at the edge of the well, and, face to face, hoisted the body.

"Mother Lecacheur and Céleste watched us from a distance, concealed behind the wall of the house. When they saw, issuing from the well, the black slippers and white stockings of the drowned person, they disappeared.

"Sapeur seized the ankles of the poor chaste woman, and we drew it up, inclined, as it was, in the most immodest posture. The head was in a shocking state, bruised and black; and the long, gray hair, hanging down, was tangled and disordered.

" 'In the name of all that is holy, how lean she is!' exclaimed Sapeur, in a contemptuous tone.

"We carried her into the room, and as the women did not put in an appearance, I, with the assistance of the lad, dressed the corpse for burial.

"I washed her disfigured face. By the touch of my hand an eye was slightly opened; it seemed to scan me with that pale stare, with that cold, that terrible look which corpses have, a look which seems to come from the beyond. I plaited up, as well as I could, her disheveled hair, and I adjusted on her forehead a novel and singularly formed lock. Then I took off her dripping wet garments, baring, not without a feeling of shame, as though I had been guilty of some profanation, her shoulders and her chest, and her long arms, slim as the twigs of branches.

"I next went to fetch some flowers, corn poppies, blue beetles, marguerites, and fresh and perfumed herbs, with which to strew her funeral couch.

"Being the only person near her, it was necessary for me to perform the usual ceremonies. In a letter found in her pocket, written at the last moment, she asked that her body be buried in the village in which she had passed the last days of her life. A frightful thought then oppressed my heart. Was it not on my account that she wished to be laid at rest in this place?

"Toward the evening, all the female gossips of the locality came to view the remains of the defunct; but I would not allow a single person to enter; I wanted to be alone; and I watched by the corpse the whole night.

"By the flickering light of the candles, I looked at the body of this miserable woman, wholly unknown, who had died so lamentably and so far away from home. Had she left no friends, no relatives behind her? What had her infancy been? What had been her life? When had she come thither, all alone, a wanderer, like a dog driven from home? What secrets of suffering and of despair were sealed up in that disagreeable body, in that spent and withered body, that impenetrable hiding place of a mystery which had driven her far away from affection and from love?

"How many unhappy beings there are! I felt that upon that human creature weighed the eternal injustice of implacable nature! Life was over with her, without her ever having experienced, perhaps, that which sustains the most miserable of us all—to wit, the hope of being once loved! Otherwise, why should she thus have concealed herself, have fled from the face of others? Why did she love everything so tenderly and so passionately, everything living that was not a man?

"I recognized, also, that she believed in a God, and that she hoped for compensation from him for the miseries she had endured. She had now begun to decompose, and to become, in turn, a plant. She who had blossomed in the sun was now to be eaten up by the cattle, carried away in herbs, and in the flesh of beasts, again to become human flesh. But that which is called the soul had been extinguished at the bottom of the dark well. She suffered no longer. She had changed her life for that of others yet to be born.

"Hours passed away in this silent and sinister communion with the dead. A pale light at length announced the dawn of a new day, and a bright ray glistened on the bed, shedding a dash of fire on the bedclothes and on her hands. This was the hour she had so much loved, when the waking birds began to sing in the trees.

"I opened the window to its fullest extent, I drew back the curtains, so that the whole heavens might look in upon us. Then bending toward the glassy corpse, I took in my hands the mutilated head, and slowly, without

terror or disgust, imprinted a long, long kiss upon those lips which had
never before received the salute of love."

*   *   *

Léon Chenal remained silent. The women wept. We heard on the box
seat Count d'Etraille blow his nose, from time to time. The coachman
alone had gone to sleep. The horses, which felt no longer the sting of the
whip, had slackened their pace and dragged softly along. And the four-in-
hand, hardly moving at all, became suddenly torpid, as if laden with
sorrow.

A Way to Wealth

"Do you know what has become of Leremy?"
"He is captain of the Sixth Dragoons."
"And Pinson?"
"Subprefect."
"And Racollet?"
"Dead."
We hunted up other names which recalled to us young figures crowned
with caps trimmed with gold braid. Later, we found some of these com-
rades, bearded, bald, married, the fathers of many children; and these
meetings, these changes, gave us some disagreeable shivers, as they
showed us how short life is, how quickly everything changes and passes
away.
My friend asked: "And Patience, the great Patience?"
I roared.
"Oh! If you want to hear about him, listen to me: Four or five weeks ago,
as traveling inspector at Limoges, I was awaiting the dinner hour. Seated
before the *Grand Café* in Theater Square, I closed my eyes wearily. The
tradesmen were coming in, in twos, or threes, or fours, taking their
absinthe or vermouth, talking in a loud voice of their business and that of
others, laughing violently, or lowering their voices when they communi-
cated something important or delicate.
"I said to myself: 'What am I going to do after dinner?' And I thought of
the long evening in this provincial town, of the slow, uninteresting walks

through the unknown streets, of the overwhelming sadness which takes possession of the solitary traveler, of the people who pass, strangers in all things and through all things, the cut of their provincial coats, their hats, their trousers, their customs, local accent, their houses, shops and carriages of singular shape. And then the ordinary sounds to which one is not accustomed; the harassing sadness which presses itself upon you little by little until you feel as if you were lost in a dangerous country, which oppresses you and makes you wish yourself back at the hotel, the hideous hotel, where your room preserves a thousand suspicious odors, where the bed makes one hesitate and the basin has a hair glued in the dirt at the bottom.

"I thought about all this as I watched them light the gas, feeling my isolated distress increase by the falling of the shadows. What was I going to do after dinner? I was alone, entirely alone, and lamentably lonesome.

"A big man came in, seated himself at a neighboring table, and commanded in a formidable voice:

" 'Waiter, my bitters.'

"The 'my' in the phrase sounded like the report of a cannon. I understood immediately that everything in existence was his, belonged to him and not to any other, that he had his character, and, by Jove! his appetite, his pantaloons, his no matter what, after his own fashion, absolute, and more complete than important. He looked about him with a satisfied air. They brought him his bitters and he called:

" 'My paper.'

"I asked myself: 'Which is his paper, I wonder?' The name of that would certainly reveal to me his opinions, his theories, his hobbies, and his nature.

"The writer brought the 'Times.' I was surprised. Why the 'Times,' a grave, somber, doctrinal, heavy journal? I thought:

" 'He is then a wise man, of serious ways, regular habits, in short, a good commoner.'

"He placed on his nose some gold eyeglasses, turned around and, before commencing to read, cast another glance all around the room. He noticed me and immediately began to look at me in a persistent, uneasy fashion. I was on the point of asking him the reason for his attention, when he cried out from where he sat:

" 'By my pipe, if it is not Gontran Lardois!'

"I answered: 'Yes, sir, you have not deceived yourself.'

"Then he got up brusquely and came toward me with outstretched hands.

" 'Ah! my old friend, how are you?' asked he.

"My greeting was constrained, not knowing him at all. Finally I stammered:

" 'Why—very well—and you?'

"He began to laugh: 'It appears that you do not know me.'

" 'No, not quite—It seems to me—however—'

"He tapped me on the shoulder:

" 'There, there! Not to bother you any longer, I am Patience, Robert Patience, your chum, your comrade.'

"I recognized him. Yes, Robert Patience, my comrade at college. It was no other. I pressed the hand he extended to me and said:

" 'Everything going well with you?'

" 'With me? Like a charm.'

"His laugh rang with triumph. He inquired:

" 'What has brought you here?'

"I explained to him that I was inspector of finances, making the rounds.

"He replied, observing my badge: 'Then you are successful?'

"I replied: 'Yes, rather; and you?'

" 'Oh! I? Very, very!'

" 'What are you doing now?'

" 'I am in business.'

" 'Then you are making money?'

" 'Lots of it. I am rich. But, come to lunch with me to-morrow at noon, No. 17 Coq-qui-chante street; then you will see my place.'

"He appeared to hesitate a second, then continued:

" 'You are still the good rounder of former times?'

" 'Yes,—I hope so.'

" 'Not married?'

" 'No.'

" 'So much the better. And you are still as fond of fun and potatoes?'

"I commenced to find him deplorably commonplace. I answered, nevertheless: 'Yes.'

" 'And pretty girls?'

" 'As to that, yes.'

"He began to laugh, with a good, hearty laugh:

" 'So much the better, so much the better,' said he. 'You recall our first farce at Bordeaux, when we had supper at the Roupie coffeehouse? Ha! what a night!'

"I recalled that night, surely; and the memory of it amused me. Other facts were brought to mind, and still others. One would say:

" 'Do you remember the time we shut up the fawn in Father Latoque's cellar?'

"And he would laugh, striking his fist upon the table, repeating:

" 'Yes—yes—yes—and you remember the mouth of the professor in geography, M. Marin, when we sent off a cracker on the map of the world just as he was orating on the principal volcanoes of the earth?'

"Then brusquely, I asked him:

" 'And you, are you married?'

"He cried: 'For ten years, my dear fellow, and I have four children, most astonishing monkeys; but you will see them and their mother.'

"We were talking loud; the neighbors were looking around at us in astonishment. Suddenly my friend looked at his watch, a chronometer as large as a citron, and cried out:

" 'Thunder! It is rude, but I shall have to leave you; I am not free this evening.'

"He rose, took both my hands and shook them as if he wished to break off my arms, and said:

" 'To-morrow at noon, you remember?'

" 'I remember.'

"I passed the morning at work at the house of the General-Treasurer. He wished to keep me for luncheon, but I told him that I had an appointment with a friend. He accompanied me out. I asked him:

" 'Do you know where Coq-qui-chante street is?'

"He answered: 'Yes, it is five minutes from here. As I have nothing to do, I will conduct you there.'

"And we set out on the way. Soon, I noticed the street we sought. It was wide, pretty enough, at the border of the town and the country. I noticed the houses and perceived number 17. It was a kind of hotel with a garden at the back. The front, ornamented with frescoes in the Italian fashion, appeared to me in bad taste. There were goddesses hanging onto urns, and others whose secret beauties a cloud concealed. Two stone Cupids held up the number.

"I said to the Treasurer: 'Here is where I am going.'

"And I extended my hand by way of leaving him. He made a brusque and singular gesture, but said nothing, pressing the hand held out to him. I rang. A maid appeared. I said:

" 'M. Patience, if you please. Is he at home?'

"She replied: 'He is here, sir—Do you wish to speak with him?'

" 'Yes.'

"The vestibule was ornamented with paintings from the brush of some local artist. Paul and Virginia were embracing under some palms drowned in a rosy light. A hideous Oriental lantern hung from the ceiling. There were many doors, masked by showy hangings. But that which struck me particularly was the odor—a permeating, perfumed odor, recalling rice powder and the moldiness of cellars—an indefinable odor in a heavy atmosphere, as overwhelming as stifling, in which the human body becomes petrified. I ascended, behind the maid, a marble staircase which was covered by a carpet of some Oriental kind, and was led into a sumptuous drawing-room.

"Left alone, I looked about me.

"The room was richly furnished, but with the pretension of an ill-bred parvenu. The engravings of the last century were pretty enough, representing women with high, powdered hair and very low-cut bodices surprised by gallant gentlemen in interesting postures. Another lady was lying on a great bed, toying with her foot with a little dog drowned in draperies. Another resisted her lover complacently, whose hand was in a suspicious place. One design showed four feet whose bodies could be divined, although concealed behind a curtain. The vast room, surrounded by soft divans, was entirely impregnated with this enervating odor, which had already taken hold of me. There was something suspicious about these walls, these stuffs, this exaggerated luxury, in short, the whole place.

"I approached the window to look into the garden, of which I could see but the trees. It was large, shady, superb. A broad path was outlined on the turf, where a jet of water was playing in the air, brought in under some masonry some distance off. And suddenly three women appeared down there, at the end of the garden, between two shapely shrubs. They were walking slowly, taking hold of each other's arms, clothed in long white dresses clouded with lace. Two of them were blonde and the other a brunette.

"They disappeared immediately among the trees. I remained transfixed, charmed, before this short but delightful apparition, which brought surging to my mind a whole poetic world. They were scarcely to be seen at all in that bower of leaves, at the end of the park, so secluded and delicious. I must have dreamed, and these were the beautiful ladies of the last century wandering under the elmtree hedge, the ladies whose light loves the clever gravures on the walls recalled. And I thought of those happy times, flowery, incorporeal, tender, when customs were so sweet and lips so easy—

"A great voice behind me made me leap back into the room. Patience had come in, radiant, extending both his hands.

"He looked at me out of the end of his eyes with the sly air of some amorous confidence and, with a large, comprehensive gesture, a Napoleonic gesture, pointed out his sumptuous drawing-room, his park, with the three women passing again at the back, and in a triumphant voice that sang of pride, said:

" 'And when you think that I commenced with nothing—my wife and my sisters-in-law!' "

My Uncle Jules

A WHITE-HAIRED OLD MAN begged us for alms. My companion, Joseph Davranche, gave him five francs. Noticing my surprised look, he said:

"That poor unfortunate reminds me of a story which I shall tell you, the memory of which continually pursues me. Here it is:

"My family, which came originally from Havre, was not rich. We just managed to make both ends meet. My father worked hard, came home late from the office, and earned very little. I had two sisters.

"My mother suffered a good deal from our reduced circumstances, and she often had harsh words for her husband, veiled and sly reproaches. The poor man then made a gesture which used to distress me. He would pass his open hand over his forehead, as if to wipe away perspiration which did not exist, and he would answer nothing. I felt his helpless suffering. We economized on everything, and never would accept an invitation to dinner, so as not to have to return the courtesy. All our provisions were bought at bargain sales. My sisters made their own gowns, and long discussions would arise on the price of a piece of braid worth fifteen centimes a yard. Our meals usually consisted of soup and beef prepared with every kind of sauce. They say it is wholesome and nourishing, but I should have preferred a change.

"I used to go through terrible scenes on account of lost buttons and torn trousers.

"Every Sunday, dressed in our best, we would take our walk along the breakwater. My father, in a frock coat, high hat and kid gloves, would offer his arm to my mother, decked out and beribboned like a ship on a holiday. My sisters, who were always ready first, would await the signal for leaving; but at the last minute some one always found a spot on my father's frock coat, and it had to be wiped away quickly with a rag moistened with benzine.

"My father, in his shirt sleeves, his silk hat on his head, would await the completion of the operation, while my mother, putting on her spectacles, and taking off her gloves in order not to spoil them, would make haste.

"Then we set out ceremoniously. My sisters marched on ahead, arm in arm. They were of marriageable age and had to be displayed. I walked on the left of my mother and my father on her right. I remember the pompous

94

air of my poor parents in these Sunday walks, their stern expression, their stiff walk. They moved slowly, with a serious expression, their bodies straight, their legs stiff, as if something of extreme importance depended upon their appearance.

"Every Sunday, when the big steamers were returning from unknown and distant countries, my father would invariably utter the same words:

" 'What a surprise it would be if Jules were on that one! Eh?'

"My Uncle Jules, my father's brother, was the only hope of the family, after being its only fear. I had heard about him since childhood, and it seemed to me that I should recognize him immediately, knowing as much about him as I did. I knew every detail of his life up to the day of his departure for America, although this period of his life was spoken of only in hushed tones.

"It seems that he had led a bad life, that is to say, he had squandered a little money, which action, in a poor family, is one of the greatest crimes. With rich people a man who amuses himself only *sows his wild oats*. He is what is generally called a *sport*. But among needy families a boy who forces his parents to break into the capital becomes a good-for-nothing, a rascal, a scamp. And this distinction is just, although the action be the same, for consequences alone determine the seriousness of the act.

"Well, Uncle Jules had visibly diminished the inheritance on which my father had counted, after he had swallowed his own to the last penny. Then, according to the custom of the times, he had been shipped off to America on a freighter going from Havre to New York.

"Once there, my uncle began to sell something or other, and he soon wrote that he was making a little money and that he soon hoped to be able to indemnify my father for the harm he had done him. This letter caused a profound emotion in the family. Jules, who up to that time had not been worth his salt, suddenly became a good man, a kind-hearted fellow, true and honest like all the Davranches.

"One of the captains told us that he had rented a large shop and was doing an important business.

"Two years later a second letter came, saying: 'My dear Philippe, I am writing to tell you not to worry about my health, which is excellent. Business is good. I leave to-morrow for a long trip to South America. I may be away for several years without sending you any news. If I shouldn't write, don't worry. When my fortune is made I shall return to Havre. I hope that it will not be too long and that we shall all live happily together. . . .'

"This letter became the gospel of the family. It was read on the slightest provocation, and it was shown to everybody.

"For ten years nothing was heard from Uncle Jules; but as time went on my father's hope grew, and my mother, also, often said:

" 'When that good Jules is here, our position will be different. There is one who knew how to get along!'

"And every Sunday, while watching the big steamers approaching from the horizon, pouring out a stream of smoke, my father would repeat his eternal question:

" 'What a surprise it would be if Jules were on that one! Eh?'

"We almost expected to see him waving his handkerchief and crying:

" 'Hey! Philippe!'

"Thousands of schemes had been planned on the strength of this expected return; we were even to buy a little house with my uncle's money—a little place in the country near Ingouville. In fact, I wouldn't swear that my father had not already begun negotiations.

"The elder of my sisters was then twenty-eight, the other twenty-six. They were not yet married, and that was a great grief to every one.

"At last a suitor presented himself for the younger one. He was a clerk, not rich, but honorable. I have always been morally certain that Uncle Jules' letter, which was shown him one evening, had swept away the young man's hesitation and definitely decided him.

"He was accepted eagerly, and it was decided that after the wedding the whole family should take a trip to Jersey.

"Jersey is the ideal trip for poor people. It is not far; one crosses a strip of sea in a steamer and lands on foreign soil, as this little island belongs to England. Thus, a Frenchman, with a two hours' sail, can observe a neighboring people at home and study their customs.

"This trip to Jersey completely absorbed our ideas, was our sole anticipation, the constant thought of our minds.

"At last we left. I see it as plainly as if it had happened yesterday. The boat was getting up steam against the quay at Granville; my father, bewildered, was superintending the loading of our three pieces of baggage; my mother, nervous, had taken the arm of my unmarried sister, who seemed lost since the departure of the other one, like the last chicken of a brood; behind us came the bride and groom, who always stayed behind, a thing that often made me turn round.

"The whistle sounded. We got on board, and the vessel, leaving the breakwater, forged ahead through a sea as flat as a marble table. We watched the coast disappear in the distance, happy and proud, like all who do not travel much.

"My father was swelling out his chest in the breeze, beneath his frock coat, which had that morning been very carefully cleaned; and he spread around him that odor of benzine which always made me recognize Sunday. Suddenly he noticed two elegantly dressed ladies to whom two gentlemen were offering oysters. An old, ragged sailor was opening them with his knife and passing them to the gentlemen, who would then offer them to the ladies. They ate them in a dainty manner, holding the shell on a fine handkerchief and advancing their mouths a little in order not to spot their dresses. Then they would drink the liquid with a rapid little motion and throw the shell overboard.

"My father was probably pleased with this delicate manner of eating oysters on a moving ship. He considered it good form, refined, and, going up to my mother and sisters, he asked:

" 'Would you like me to offer you some oysters?'

"My mother hesitated on account of the expense, but my two sisters immediately accepted. My mother said in a provoked manner:

" 'I am afraid that they will hurt my stomach. Offer the children some, but not too much, it would make them sick.' Then, turning toward me, she added:

" 'As for Joseph, he doesn't need any. Boys shouldn't be spoiled.'

"However, I remained beside my mother, finding this discrimination unjust. I watched my father as he pompously conducted my two sisters and his son-in-law toward the ragged old sailor.

"The two ladies had just left, and my father showed my sisters how to eat them without spilling the liquor. He even tried to give them an example, and seized an oyster. He attempted to imitate the ladies, and immediately spilled all the liquid over his coat. I heard my mother mutter:

" 'He would do far better to keep quiet.'

"But, suddenly, my father appeared to be worried; he retreated a few steps, stared at his family gathered around the old shell opener, and quickly came toward us. He seemed very pale, with a peculiar look. In a low voice he said to my mother:

" 'It's extraordinary how that man opening the oysters looks like Jules.'

"Astonished, my mother asked:

" 'What Jules?'

"My father continued:

" 'Why, my brother. If I did not know that he was well off in America, I should think it was he.'

"Bewildered, my mother stammered:

" 'You are crazy! As long as you know that it is not he, why do you say such foolish things?'

"But my father insisted:

" 'Go on over and see, Clarisse! I would rather have you see with your own eyes.'

"She arose and walked to her daughters. I, too, was watching the man. He was old, dirty, wrinkled, and did not lift his eyes from his work.

"My mother returned. I noticed that she was trembling. She exclaimed quickly:

" 'I believe that it is he. Why don't you ask the captain? But be very careful that we don't have this rogue on our hands again!'

"My father walked away, but I followed him. I felt strangely moved.

"The captain, a tall, thin man, with blond whiskers, was walking along the bridge with an important air as if he were commanding the Indian mail steamer.

"My father addressed him ceremoniously, and questioned him about his profession, adding many compliments:

" 'What might be the importance of Jersey? What did it produce? What was the population? The customs? The nature of the soil?' etc., etc.

" 'You have there an old shell opener who seems quite interesting. Do you know anything about him?'

"The captain, whom this conversation began to weary, answered dryly:

" 'He is some old French tramp whom I found last year in America, and I brought him back. It seems that he has some relatives in Havre, but that he doesn't wish to return to them because he owes them money. His name is Jules—Jules Darmanche or Darvanche or something like that. It seems that he was once rich over there, but you can see what's left of him now.'

"My father turned ashy pale and muttered, his throat contracted, his eyes haggard:

" 'Ah! ah! very well, very well. I'm not in the least surprised. Thank you very much, Captain.'

"He went away, and the astonished sailor watched him disappear. He returned to my mother so upset that she said to him:

" 'Sit down; some one will notice that something is the matter.'

"He sank down on a bench and stammered:

" 'It's he! It's he!'

"Then he asked:

" 'What are we going to do?'

"She answered quickly:

" 'We must get the children out of the way. Since Joseph knows everything, he can go and get them. We must take good care that our son-in-law doesn't find out.'

"My father seemed absolutely bewildered. He murmured:

" 'What a catastrophe!'

"Suddenly growing furious, my mother exclaimed:

" 'I always thought that that thief never would do anything, and that he would drop down on us again! As if one could expect anything from a Davranche!'

"My father passed his hand over his forehead, as he always did when his wife reproached him. She added:

" 'Give Joseph some money so that he can pay for the oysters. All that it would need to cap the climax would be to be recognized by that beggar. That would be very pleasant! Let's get down to the other end of the boat, and take care that that man doesn't come near us!'

"They gave me five francs and walked away.

"Astonished, my sisters were awaiting their father. I said that mamma had felt a sudden attack of sea-sickness, and I asked the shell opener:

" 'How much do we owe you, monsieur?'

"I felt like laughing: he was my uncle! He answered:

" 'Two francs fifty.'

"I held out my five francs and he returned the change. I looked at his hand; it was a poor, wrinkled, sailor's hand, and I looked at his face, an unhappy old face. I said to myself:

" 'That is my uncle, the brother of my father, my uncle!'

"I gave him a ten-cent tip. He thanked me:

" 'God bless you, my young sir!'

"He spoke like a poor man receiving alms. I couldn't help thinking that he must have begged over there! My sisters looked at me, surprised at my generosity. When I returned the two francs to my father, my mother asked me in surprise:

" 'Was there three francs' worth? That is impossible.'

"I answered in a firm voice:

" 'I gave ten cents as a tip.'

"My mother started, and, staring at me, she exclaimed:

" 'You must be crazy! Give ten cents to that man, to that vagabond——'

"She stopped at a look from my father, who was pointing at his son-in-law. Then everybody was silent.

"Before us, on the distant horizon, a purple shadow seemed to rise out of the sea. It was Jersey.

"As we approached the breakwater a violent desire seized me once more to see my Uncle Jules, to be near him, to say to him something consoling, something tender. But as no one was eating any more oysters, he had disappeared, having probably gone below to the dirty hold which was the home of the poor wretch."

The Horla

MAY 8. What a lovely day! I have spent all the morning lying in the grass in front of my house, under the enormous plane tree that shades the whole of it. I like this part of the country and I like to live here because I am attached to it by old associations, by those deep and delicate roots which attach a man to the soil on which his ancestors were born and died, which attach him to the ideas and usages of the place as well as to the food, to local expressions, to the peculiar twang of the peasants, to the smell of the soil, of the villages and of the atmosphere itself.

I love my house in which I grew up. From my windows I can see the Seine which flows alongside my garden, on the other side of the high road, almost through my grounds, the great and wide Seine, which goes to Rouen and Havre, and is covered with boats passing to and fro.

On the left, down yonder, lies Rouen, that large town, with its blue roofs, under its pointed Gothic towers. These are innumerable, slender or broad, dominated by the spire of the cathedral, and full of bells which sound through the blue air on fine mornings, sending their sweet and distant iron clang even as far as my home; that song of the metal, which the breeze wafts in my direction, now stronger and now weaker, according as the wind is stronger or lighter.

What a delicious morning it was!

About eleven o'clock, a long line of boats drawn by a steam tug as big as a fly, and which scarcely puffed while emitting its thick smoke, passed my gate.

After two English schooners, whose red flag fluttered in space, there came a magnificent Brazilian three-master; it was perfectly white, and wonderfully clean and shining. I saluted it, I hardly knew why, except that the sight of the vessel gave me great pleasure.

May 12. I have had a slight feverish attack for the last few days, and I feel ill, or rather I feel low-spirited.

Whence come those mysterious influences which change our happiness into discouragement, and our self-confidence into diffidence? One might almost say that the air, the invisible air, is full of unknowable Powers whose mysterious presence we have to endure. I wake up in the best spirits, with an inclination to sing. Why? I go down to the edge of the water, and suddenly, after walking a short distance, I return home wretched, as if some misfortune were awaiting me there. Why? Is it a cold shiver which, passing over my skin, has upset my nerves and given me low spirits? Is it the form of the clouds, the color of the sky, or the color of the surrounding objects which is so changeable, that has troubled my thoughts as they passed before my eyes? Who can tell? Everything that surrounds us, everything that we see, without looking at it, everything that we touch, without knowing it, everything that we handle, without feeling it, all that we meet, without clearly distinguishing it, has a rapid, surprising and inexplicable effect upon us and upon our senses, and, through them, on our ideas and on our heart itself.

How profound that mystery of the Invisible is! We cannot fathom it with our miserable senses, with our eyes which are unable to perceive what is either too small or too great, too near to us, or too far from us—neither the inhabitants of a star nor of a drop of water; nor with our ears that deceive us, for they transmit to us the vibrations of the air in sonorous notes. They are fairies who work the miracle of changing these vibrations into sound, and by that metamorphosis give birth to music, which makes the silent motion of nature musical . . . with our sense of smell which is less keen than that of a dog . . . with our sense of taste which can scarcely distinguish the age of a wine!

Oh! If we only had other organs which would work other miracles in our favor, what a number of fresh things we might discover around us!

May 16. I am ill, decidedly! I was so well last month! I am feverish, horribly feverish, or rather I am in a state of feverish enervation, which makes my mind suffer as much as my body. I have, continually, that horrible sensation of some impending danger, that apprehension of some coming misfortune, or of approaching death; that presentiment which is, no doubt, an attack of some illness which is still unknown, which germinates in the flesh and in the blood.

May 17. I have just come from consulting my physician, for I could no longer get any sleep. He said my pulse was rapid, my eyes dilated, my nerves highly strung, but there were no alarming symptoms. I must take a course of shower baths and of bromide of potassium.

May 25. No change! My condition is really very peculiar. As the evening comes on, an incomprehensible feeling of disquietude seizes me, just as if night concealed some threatening disaster. I dine hurriedly, and then try to read, but I do not understand the words, and can scarcely distinguish the letters. Then I walk up and down my drawing-room, oppressed by a feeling of confused and irresistible fear, the fear of sleep and fear of my bed.

About ten o'clock I go up to my room. As soon as I enter it I double-lock and bolt the door; I am afraid . . . of what? Up to the present time I have been afraid of nothing . . . I open my cupboards, and look under my bed; I listen . . . to what? How strange it is that a simple feeling of discomfort, impeded or heightened circulation, perhaps the irritation of a nerve filament, a slight congestion, a small disturbance in the imperfect delicate functioning of our living machinery, may turn the most light-hearted of men into a melancholy one, and make a coward of the bravest? Then, I go to bed, and wait for sleep as a man might wait for the executioner. I wait for its coming with dread, and my heart beats and my legs tremble, while my whole body shivers beneath the warmth of the bedclothes, until all at once I fall asleep, as though one should plunge into a pool of stagnant water in order to drown. I do not feel it coming on as I did formerly, this perfidious sleep which is close to me and watching me, which is going to seize me by the head, to close my eyes and annihilate me.

I sleep—a long time—two or three hours perhaps—then a dream—no—a nightmare lays hold on me. I feel that I am in bed and asleep . . . I feel it and I know it . . . and I feel also that somebody is coming close to me, is looking at me, touching me, is getting on to my bed, is kneeling on my chest, is taking my neck between his hands and squeezing it . . . squeezing it with all his might in order to strangle me.

I struggle, bound by that terrible sense of powerlessness which para-lyzes us in our dreams; I try to cry out—but I cannot; I want to move—I cannot do so; I try, with the most violent efforts and breathing hard, to turn over and throw off this being who is crushing and suffocating me—I cannot!

And then, suddenly, I wake up, trembling and bathed in perspiration; I light a candle and find that I am alone, and after that crisis, which occurs every night, I at length fall asleep and slumber tranquilly till morning.

June 2. My condition has grown worse. What is the matter with me? The bromide does me no good, and the shower baths have no effect. Some-times, in order to tire myself thoroughly, though I am fatigued enough already, I go for a walk in the forest of Roumare. I used to think at first that the fresh light and soft air, impregnated with the odor of herbs and leaves, would instill new blood into my veins and impart fresh energy to my heart. I turned into a broad hunting road, and then turned toward La Bouille, through a narrow path, between two rows of exceedingly tall trees, which placed a thick green, almost black, roof between the sky and me.

A sudden shiver ran through me, not a cold shiver, but a strange shiver of agony, and I hastened my steps, uneasy at being alone in the forest, afraid, stupidly and without reason, of the profound solitude. Suddenly it seemed to me as if I were being followed, that somebody was walking at my heels, close, quite close to me, near enough to touch me.

I turned round suddenly, but I was alone. I saw nothing behind me except the straight, broad path, empty and bordered by high trees, horribly empty; before me it also extended until it was lost in the distance, and looked just the same, terrible.

I closed my eyes. Why? And then I began to turn round on one heel very quickly, just like a top. I nearly fell down, and opened my eyes; the trees were dancing round me and the earth heaved; I was obliged to sit down. Then, ah! I no longer remembered how I had come! What a strange idea! What a strange, strange idea! I did not the least know. I started off to the right, and got back into the avenue which had led me into the middle of the forest.

June 3. I have had a terrible night. I shall go away for a few weeks, for no doubt a journey will set me up again.

July 2. I have come back, quite cured, and have had a most delightful trip into the bargain. I have been to Mont Saint-Michel, which I had not seen before.

What a sight, when one arrives as I did, at Avranches toward the end of the day! The town stands on a hill, and I was taken into the public garden at the extremity of the town. I uttered a cry of astonishment. An extraordinarily large bay lay extended before me, as far as my eyes could reach, between two hills which were lost to sight in the mist; and in the middle of this immense yellow bay, under a clear, golden sky, a peculiar hill rose up, sombre and pointed in the midst of the sand. The sun had just disappeared, and under the still flaming sky appeared the outline of that fantastic rock which bears on its summit a fantastic monument.

At daybreak I went out to it. The tide was low, as it had been the night before, and I saw that wonderful abbey rise up before me as I approached it. After several hours' walking, I reached the enormous mass of rocks which supports the little town, dominated by the great church. Having climbed the steep and narrow street, I entered the most wonderful Gothic building that has ever been built to God on earth, as large as a town, full of low rooms which seem buried beneath vaulted roofs, and lofty galleries supported by delicate columns.

I entered this gigantic granite gem, which is as light as a bit of lace, covered with towers, with slender belfries with spiral staircases, which raise their strange heads that bristle with chimeras, with devils, with fantastic animals, with monstrous flowers, to the blue sky by day, and to the black sky by night, and are connected by finely carved arches.

When I had reached the summit I said to the monk who accompanied me: "Father, how happy you must be here!" And he replied: "It is very windy here, monsieur"; and so we began to talk while watching the rising tide, which ran over the sand and covered it as with a steel cuirass.

And then the monk told me stories, all the old stories belonging to the place, legends, nothing but legends.

One of them struck me forcibly. The country people, those belonging to the Mount, declare that at night one can hear voices talking on the sands, and then that one hears two goats bleating, one with a strong, the other with a weak voice. Incredulous people declare that it is nothing but the cry of the sea birds, which occasionally resembles bleatings, and occasionally, human lamentations; but belated fishermen swear that they have met an old shepherd wandering between tides on the sands around the little town. His head is completely concealed by his cloak and he is followed by a billy goat with a man's face, and a nanny goat with a woman's face, both having long, white hair and talking incessantly and quarreling in an unknown tongue. Then suddenly they cease and begin to bleat with all their might.

"Do you believe it?" I asked the monk. "I scarcely know," he replied, and I continued: "If there are other beings besides ourselves on this earth, how comes it that we have not known it long since, or why have *you* not seen them? How is it that *I* have not seen them?" He replied: "Do we see the hundred-thousandth part of what exists? Look here; there is the wind, which is the strongest force in nature, which knocks down men, and blows down buildings, uproots trees, raises the sea into mountains of water, destroys cliffs and casts great ships on the rocks; the wind which kills, which whistles, which sighs, which roars—have you ever seen it, and can you see it? It exists for all that, however."

I was silent before this simple reasoning. That man was a philosopher, or perhaps a fool; I could not say which exactly, so I held my tongue. What he had said had often been in my own thoughts.

July 3. I have slept badly; certainly there is some feverish influence here, for my coachman is suffering in the same way as I am. When I went back home yesterday, I noticed his singular paleness, and I asked him: "What is the matter with you, Jean?" "The matter is that I never get any rest, and my nights devour my days. Since your departure, monsieur, there has been a spell over me."

However, the other servants are all well, but I am very much afraid of having another attack myself.

July 4. I am decidedly ill again; for my old nightmares have returned. Last night I felt somebody leaning on me and sucking my life from between my lips. Yes, he was sucking it out of my throat, like a leech. Then he got up, satiated, and I woke up, so exhausted, crushed and weak that I could not move. If this continues for a few days, I shall certainly go away again.

July 5. Have I lost my reason? What happened last night is so strange that my head wanders when I think of it!

I had locked my door, as I do now every evening, and then, being thirsty, I drank half a glass of water, and accidentally noticed that the water bottle was full up to the cut-glass stopper.

Then I went to bed and fell into one of my terrible sleeps, from which I was aroused in about two hours by a still more frightful shock.

Picture to yourself a sleeping man who is being murdered and who wakes up with a knife in his lung, and whose breath rattles, who is covered with blood, and who can no longer breathe and is about to die, and does not understand—there you have it.

Having recovered my senses, I was thirsty again, so I lit a candle and went to the table on which stood my water bottle. I lifted it up and tilted it over my glass, but nothing came out. It was empty! It was completely empty! At first I could not understand it at all, and then suddenly I was seized by such a terrible feeling that I had to sit down, or rather I fell into a chair! Then I sprang up suddenly to look about me; then I sat down again, overcome by astonishment and fear, in front of the transparent glass bottle! I looked at it with fixed eyes, trying to conjecture, and my hands trembled! Somebody had drunk the water, but who? I? I without any doubt. It could surely only be I. In that case I was a somnambulist; I lived, without knowing it, that mysterious double life which makes us doubt whether there are not two beings in us, or whether a strange, unknowable and invisible being does not at such moments, when our soul is in a state of torpor, animate our captive body, which obeys this other being, as it obeys us, and more than it obeys ourselves.

Oh! Who will understand my horrible agony? Who will understand the emotion of a man who is sound in mind, wide awake, full of common sense, who looks in horror through the glass of a water bottle for a little water that disappeared while he was asleep? I remained thus until it was daylight, without venturing to go to bed again.

July 6. I am going mad. Again all the contents of my water bottle have been drunk during the night—or rather, I have drunk it!

But is it I? Is it I? Who could it be? Who? Oh! God! Am I going mad? Who will save me?

July 10. I have just been through some surprising ordeals. Decidedly I am mad! And yet! . . .

On July 6, before going to bed, I put some wine, milk, water, bread and strawberries on my table. Somebody drank—I drank—all the water and a little of the milk, but neither the wine, bread, nor the strawberries were touched.

On the seventh of July I renewed the same experiment, with the same results, and on July 8, I left out the water and the milk, and nothing was touched.

Lastly, on July 9, I put only water and milk on my table, taking care to wrap up the bottles in white muslin and to tie down the stoppers. Then I rubbed my lips, my beard and my hands with pencil lead, and went to bed.

Irresistible sleep seized me, which was soon followed by a terrible awakening. I had not moved, and there was no mark of lead on the sheets. I rushed to the table. The muslin round the bottles remained intact; I undid the string, trembling with fear. All the water had been drunk, and so had the milk! Ah! Great God! . . .

I must start for Paris immediately.

July 12. Paris. I must have lost my head during the last few days! I must be the plaything of my enervated imagination, unless I am really a somnambulist, or that I have been under the power of one of those hitherto unexplained influences which are called suggestions. In any case, my mental state bordered on madness, and twenty-four hours of Paris sufficed to restore my equilibrium.

Yesterday, after doing some business and paying some visits which instilled fresh and invigorating air into my soul, I wound up the evening at the *Théâtre-Français*. A play by Alexandre Dumas the younger was being acted, and his active and powerful imagination completed my cure. Certainly solitude is dangerous for active minds. We require around us men who can think and talk. When we are alone for a long time, we people space with phantoms.

I returned along the boulevards to my hotel in excellent spirits. Amid the jostling of the crowd I thought, not without irony, of my terrors and surmises of the previous week, because I had believed—yes, I had believed—that an invisible being lived beneath my roof. How weak our brains are, and how quickly they are terrified and led into error by a small incomprehensible fact.

Instead of saying simply: "I do not understand because I do not know the cause," we immediately imagine terrible mysteries and supernatural powers.

July 14. Fête of the Republic. I walked through the streets, amused as a child at the firecrackers and flags. Still it is very foolish to be merry on a fixed date, by Government decree. The populace is an imbecile flock of sheep, now stupidly patient, and now in ferocious revolt. Say to it: "Amuse yourself," and it amuses itself. Say to it: "Go and fight with your neighbor," and it goes and fights. Say to it: "Vote for the Emperor," and it votes for the Emperor, and then say to it: "Vote for the Republic," and it votes for the Republic.

Those who direct it are also stupid; only, instead of obeying men, they obey principles which can only be stupid, sterile, and false, for the very reason that they are principles, that is to say, ideas which are considered as certain and unchangeable, in this world where one is certain of nothing, since light is an illusion and noise is an illusion.

July 16. I saw some things yesterday that troubled me very much.

I was dining at the house of my cousin, Madame Sablé, whose husband is colonel of the 76th Chasseurs at Limoges. There were two young women there, one of whom had married a medical man, Dr. Parent, who devotes much attention to nervous diseases and to the remarkable manifestations taking place at this moment under the influence of hypnotism and suggestion.

He related to us at some length the wonderful results obtained by English scientists and by the doctors of the Nancy school; and the facts which he adduced appeared to me so strange that I declared that I was altogether incredulous.

"We are," he declared, "on the point of discovering one of the most important secrets of nature; I mean to say, one of its most important secrets on this earth, for there are certainly others of a different kind of importance up in the stars, yonder. Ever since man has thought, ever since he has been able to express and write down his thoughts, he has felt himself close to a mystery which is impenetrable to his gross and imperfect senses, and he endeavors to supplement through his intellect the inefficiency of his senses. As long as that intellect remained in its elementary stage, these apparitions of invisible spirits assumed forms that were commonplace, though terrifying. Thence sprang the popular belief in the supernatural, the legends of wandering spirits, of fairies, of gnomes, ghosts, I might even say the legend of God; for our conceptions of the workman-creator, from whatever religion they may have come down to us, are certainly the most mediocre, the most stupid and the most incredible inventions that ever sprang from the terrified brain of any human beings. Nothing is truer than what Voltaire says: 'God made man in His own image, but man has certainly paid Him back in his own coin.'

"However, for rather more than a century men seem to have had a presentiment of something new. Mesmer and some others have put us on an unexpected track, and, especially within the last two or three years, we have arrived at really surprising results."

My cousin, who is also very incredulous, smiled, and Dr. Parent said to her: "Would you like me to try and send you to sleep, madame?" "Yes, certainly."

She sat down in an easy chair, and he began to look at her fixedly, so as to fascinate her. I suddenly felt myself growing uncomfortable, my heart beating rapidly and a choking sensation in my throat. I saw Madame Sablé's eyes becoming heavy, her mouth twitching and her bosom heaving, and at the end of ten minutes she was asleep.

"Go behind her," the doctor said to me, and I took a seat behind her. He put a visiting card into her hands, and said to her: "This is a looking-glass; what do you see in it?" And she replied: "I see my cousin." "What is he doing?" "He is twisting his mustache." "And now?" "He is taking a photograph out of his pocket." "Whose photograph is it?" "His own."

That was true, and the photograph had been given me that same evening at the hotel.

"What is his attitude in this portrait?" "He is standing up with his hat in his hand."

She saw, therefore, on that card, on that piece of white pasteboard, as if she had seen it in a mirror.

The young women were frightened, and exclaimed: "That is enough! Quite, quite enough!"

But the doctor said to Madame Sablé authoritatively: "You will rise at eight o'clock to-morrow morning; then you will go and call on your cousin at his hotel and ask him to lend you five thousand francs which your husband demands of you, and which he will ask for when he sets out on his coming journey."

Then he woke her up.

On returning to my hotel, I thought over this curious séance, and I was assailed by doubts, not as to my cousin's absolute and undoubted good faith, for I had known her as well as if she were my own sister ever since she was a child, but as to a possible trick on the doctor's part. Had he not, perhaps, kept a glass hidden in his hand, which he showed to the young woman in her sleep, at the same time as he did the card? Professional conjurors do things that are just as singular.

So I went home and to bed, and this morning, at about half-past eight, I was awakened by my valet, who said to me: "Madame Sablé has asked to see you immediately, monsieur." I dressed hastily and went to her.

She sat down in some agitation, with her eyes on the floor, and without raising her veil she said to me: "My dear cousin, I am going to ask a great favor of you." "What is it, cousin?" "I do not like to tell you, and yet I must. I am in absolute need of five thousand francs." "What, you?" "Yes, I, or rather my husband, who has asked me to procure them for him."

I was so thunderstruck that I stammered out my answers. I asked myself whether she had not really been making fun of me with Dr. Parent, if it was not merely a very well-acted farce which had been rehearsed beforehand. On looking at her attentively, however, all my doubts disappeared. She was trembling with grief, so painful was this step to her, and I was convinced that her throat was full of sobs.

I knew that she was very rich and I continued: "What! Has not your husband five thousand francs at his disposal? Come, think. Are you sure that he commissioned you to ask me for them?"

She hesitated for a few seconds, as if she were making a great effort to search her memory, and then she replied: "Yes . . . yes, I am quite sure of it." "He has written to you?"

She hesitated again and reflected, and I guessed the torture of her thoughts. She did not know. She only knew that she was to borrow five thousand francs of me for her husband. So she told a lie. "Yes, he has written to me." "When, pray? You did not mention it to me yesterday." "I received his letter this morning." "Can you show it me?" "No; no . . . no . . . it contained private matters . . . things too personal to ourselves. . . . I burned it." "So your husband runs into debt?"

She hesitated again, and then murmured: "I do not know." Thereupon I said bluntly: "I have not five thousand francs at my disposal at this moment, my dear cousin."

She uttered a kind of cry as if she were in pain and said: "Oh! oh! I beseech you, I beseech you to get them for me. . . ."

She got excited and clasped her hands as if she were praying to me! I heard her voice change its tone; she wept and stammered, harassed and dominated by the irresistible order that she had received.

"Oh! oh! I beg you to . . . if you knew what I am suffering . . . I want them to-day."

I had pity on her: "You shall have them by and by, I swear to you." "Oh! thank you! thank you! How kind you are."

I continued: "Do you remember what took place at your house last night?" "Yes." "Do you remember that Dr. Parent sent you to sleep?" "Yes." "Oh! Very well, then; he ordered you to come to me this morning to borrow five thousand francs, and at this moment you are obeying that suggestion."

She considered for a few moments, and then replied: "But as it is my husband who wants them—"

For a whole hour I tried to convince her, but could not succeed, and when she had gone I went to the doctor. He was just going out, and he listened to me with a smile, and said: "Do you believe now?" "Yes, I cannot help it." "Let us go to your cousin's."

She was already half asleep on a reclining chair, overcome with fatigue.

The doctor felt her pulse, looked at her for some time with one hand raised toward her eyes, which she closed by degrees under the irresistible power of this magnetic influence, and when she was asleep, he said:

"Your husband does not require the five thousand francs any longer! You must, therefore, forget that you asked your cousin to lend them to you, and, if he speaks to you about it, you will not understand him."

Then he woke her up, and I took out a pocketbook and said: "Here is what you asked me for this morning, my dear cousin." But she was so surprised that I did not venture to persist; nevertheless, I tried to recall the circumstance to her, but she denied it vigorously, thought I was making fun of her, and, in the end, very nearly lost her temper.

* * *

There! I have just come back, and I have not been able to eat any lunch, for this experiment has altogether upset me.

July 19. Many people to whom I told the adventure laughed at me. I no longer know what to think. The wise man says: "It may be!"

July 21. I dined at Bougival, and then I spent the evening at a boatmen's ball. Decidedly everything depends on place and surroundings. It would be the height of folly to believe in the supernatural on the Ile de la Grenouillière . . . but on the top of Mont Saint-Michel? . . . and in India? We are terribly influenced by our surroundings. I shall return home next week.

July 30. I came back to my own house yesterday. Everything is going on well.

August 2. Nothing new; it is splendid weather, and I spend my days in watching the Seine flowing past.

August 4. Quarrels among my servants. They declare that the glasses are broken in the cupboards at night. The footman accuses the cook, who accuses the seamstress, who accuses the other two. Who is the culprit? It is a clever person who can tell.

August 6. This time I am not mad. I have seen . . . I have seen . . . I have seen! . . . I can doubt no longer . . . I have seen it! . . .

I was walking at two o'clock among my rose trees, in the full sunlight . . . in the walk bordered by autumn roses which are beginning to fall. As I stopped to look at a Géant de Bataille, which had three splendid blossoms, I distinctly saw the stalk of one of the roses near me bend, as if an invisible hand had bent it, and then break, as if that hand had picked it! Then the flower raised itself, following the curve which a hand would have described in carrying it toward a mouth, and it remained suspended in the transparent air, all alone and motionless, a terrible red spot, three yards from my eyes. In desperation I rushed at it to take it! I found nothing; it had disappeared. Then I was seized with furious rage against myself, for a reasonable and serious man should not have such hallucinations.

But was it an hallucination? I turned round to look for the stalk, and I found it at once, on the bush, freshly broken, between two other roses which remained on the branch. I returned home then, my mind greatly disturbed; for I am certain now, as certain as I am of the alternation of day and night, that there exists close to me an invisible being that lives on milk and water, that can touch objects, take them and change their places; that is, consequently, endowed with a material nature, although it is imperceptible to our senses, and that lives as I do, under my roof—

August 7. I slept tranquilly. He drank the water out of my decanter, but did not disturb my sleep.

I wonder if I am mad. As I was walking just now in the sun by the river side, doubts as to my sanity arose in me; not vague doubts such as I have had hitherto, but definite, absolute doubts. I have seen mad people, and I have known some who have been quite intelligent, lucid, even clear-sighted in every concern of life, except on one point. They spoke clearly, readily, profoundly on everything, when suddenly their mind struck upon the shoals of their madness and broke to pieces there, and scattered and floundered in that furious and terrible sea, full of rolling waves, fogs and squalls, which is called *madness*.

I certainly should think that I was mad, absolutely mad, if I were not conscious, did not perfectly know my condition, did not fathom it by analyzing it with the most complete lucidity. I should, in fact, be only a rational man who was laboring under an hallucination. Some unknown disturbance must have arisen in my brain, one of those disturbances which physiologists of the present day try to note and to verify; and that disturbance must have caused a deep gap in my mind and in the sequence and logic of my ideas. Similar phenomena occur in dreams which lead us among the most unlikely phantasmagoria, without causing us any surprise, because our verifying apparatus and our organ of control are asleep, while our imaginative faculty is awake and active. Is it not possible that one of the imperceptible notes of the cerebral keyboard has been paralyzed in me? Some men lose the recollection of proper names, of verbs, or of numbers, or merely of dates, in consequence of an accident. The localization of all the variations of thought has been established nowadays; why, then, should it be surprising if my faculty of controlling the unreality of certain hallucinations were dormant in me for the time being?

I thought of all this as I walked by the side of the water. The sun shone brightly on the river and made earth delightful, while it filled me with a love for life, for the swallows, whose agility always delights my eye, for the plants by the river side, the rustle of whose leaves is a pleasure to my ears.

By degrees, however, an inexplicable feeling of discomfort seized me. It seemed as if some unknown force were numbing and stopping me, were preventing me from going further, and were calling me back. I felt that painful wish to return which oppresses you when you have left a beloved invalid at home, and when you are seized with a presentiment that he is worse.

I, therefore, returned in spite of myself, feeling certain that I should find some bad news awaiting me, a letter or a telegram. There was nothing, however, and I was more surprised and uneasy than if I had had another fantastic vision.

August 8. I spent a terrible evening yesterday. He does not show himself any more, but I feel that he is near me, watching me, looking at me, penetrating me, dominating me, and more redoubtable when he hides himself thus than if he were to manifest his constant and invisible presence by supernatural phenomena. However, I slept.

August 9. Nothing, but I am afraid.

August 10. Nothing; what will happen to-morrow?

August 11. Still nothing; I cannot stop at home with this fear hanging over me and these thoughts in my mind; I shall go away.

August 12. Ten o'clock at night. All day long I have been trying to get away, and have not been able. I wished to accomplish this simple and easy act of freedom——to go out——to get into my carriage in order to go to Rouen——and I have not been able to do it. What is the reason?

August 13. When one is attacked by certain maladies, all the springs of our physical being appear to be broken, all our energies destroyed, all our muscles relaxed; our bones, too, have become as soft as flesh, and our blood as liquid as water. I am experiencing these sensations in my moral being in a strange and distressing manner. I have no longer any strength, any courage, any self-control, not even any power to set my own will in motion. I have no power left to will anything; but some one does it for me and I obey.

August 14. I am lost! Somebody possesses my soul and dominates it. Somebody orders all my acts, all my movements, all my thoughts. I am no longer anything in myself, nothing except an enslaved and terrified spectator of all the things I do. I wish to go out; I cannot. He does not wish to, and so I remain, trembling and distracted, in the armchair in which he keeps me sitting. I merely wish to get up and to rouse myself; I cannot! I am riveted to my chair, and my chair adheres to the ground in such a manner that no power could move us.

Then, suddenly, I must, I must go to the bottom of my garden to pick some strawberries and eat them, and I go there. I pick the strawberries and eat them! Oh, my God! My God! Is there a God? If there be one, deliver me! Save me! Succor me! Pardon! Pity! Mercy! Save me! Oh, what sufferings! What torture! What horror!

August 15. This is certainly the way in which my poor cousin was possessed and controlled when she came to borrow five thousand francs of me. She was under the power of a strange will which had entered into her, like another soul, like another parasitic and dominating soul. Is the world coming to an end?

But who is he, this invisible being that rules me? This unknowable being, this rover of a supernatural race?

Invisible beings exist, then! How is it, then, that since the beginning of the world they have never manifested themselves precisely as they do to me? I have never read of anything that resembles what goes on in my house. Oh, if I could only leave it, if I could only go away, escape, and never return! I should be saved, but I cannot.

August 16. I managed to escape to-day for two hours, like a prisoner who finds the door of his dungeon accidentally open. I suddenly felt that I was free and that he was far away, and so I gave orders to harness the horses as quickly as possible, and I drove to Rouen. Oh, how delightful to be able to say to a man who obeys you: "Go to Rouen!"

I made him pull up before the library, and I begged them to lend me Dr. Herrmann Herestauss' treatise on the unknown inhabitants of the ancient and modern world.

Then, as I was getting into my carriage, I intended to say: "To the railway station!" but instead of this I shouted—I did not say, but I shouted—in such a loud voice that all the passers-by turned round: "Home!" and I fell back on the cushion of my carriage, overcome by mental agony. He had found me again and regained possession of me.

August 17. Oh, what a night! What a night! And yet it seems to me that I ought to rejoice. I read until one o'clock in the morning! Herestauss, doctor of philosophy and theogony, wrote the history of the manifestation of all those invisible beings which hover around man, or of whom he dreams. He describes their origin, their domain, their power; but none of them resembles the one which haunts me. One might say that man, ever since he began to think, has had a foreboding fear of a new being, stronger than himself, his successor in this world, and that, feeling his presence, and not being able to foresee the nature of that master, he has, in his terror, created the whole race of occult beings, of vague phantoms born of fear.

Having, therefore, read until one o'clock in the morning, I went and sat down at the open window, in order to cool my forehead and my thoughts, in the calm night air. It was very pleasant and warm! How I should have enjoyed such a night formerly!

There was no moon, but the stars darted out their rays in the dark heavens. Who inhabits those worlds? What forms, what living beings, what animals are there yonder? What do the thinkers in those distant worlds know more than we do? What can they do more than we can? What do they see which we do not know? Will not one of them, some day or other, traversing space, appear on our earth to conquer it, just as the Norsemen formerly crossed the sea in order to subjugate nations more feeble than themselves?

We are so weak, so defenseless, so ignorant, so small, we who live on this particle of mud which revolves in a drop of water.

I fell asleep, dreaming thus in the cool night air, and when I had slept for about three-quarters of an hour, I opened my eyes without moving, awakened by I know not what confused and strange sensation. At first I saw nothing, and then suddenly it appeared to me as if a page of a book which had remained open on my table turned over of its own accord. Not a breath of air had come in at my window, and I was surprised, and waited. In about four minutes, I saw, I saw, yes, I saw with my own eyes, another page lift itself up and fall down on the others, as if a finger had turned it over. My armchair was empty, appeared empty, but I knew that he was there, he, and sitting in my place, and that he was reading. With a furious bound, the bound of an enraged wild beast that springs at its tamer, I crossed my room to seize him, to strangle him, to kill him! But before I could reach it, the chair fell over as if somebody had run away from me— my table rocked, my lamp fell and went out, and my window closed as if some thief had been surprised and had fled out into the night, shutting it behind him.

So he had run away; he had been afraid; he, afraid of me!

But—but—to-morrow—or later—some day or other—I should be able to hold him in my clutches and crush him against the ground! Do not dogs occasionally bite and strangle their masters?

August 18. I have been thinking the whole day long. Oh, yes, I will obey him, follow his impulses, fulfill all his wishes, show myself humble, submissive, a coward. He is the stronger; but the hour will come—

August 19. I know—I know—I know all! I have just read the following in the *Revue du Monde Scientifique:* "A curious piece of news comes to us from Rio de Janeiro. Madness, an epidemic of madness, which may be compared to that contagious madness which attacked the people of Europe in the Middle Ages, is at this moment raging in the Province of San-Paolo. The terrified inhabitants are leaving their houses, saying that they are pursued, possessed, dominated like human cattle by invisible, though tangible beings, a species of vampire, which feed on their life while they are asleep, and who, besides, drink water and milk without appearing to touch any other nourishment.

"Professor Don Pedro Henriques, accompanied by several medical savants, has gone to the Province of San-Paolo, in order to study the origin and the manifestations of this surprising madness on the spot, and to propose such measures to the Emperor as may appear to him to be most fitted to restore the mad population to reason."

Ah! Ah! I remember now that fine Brazilian three-master which passed in front of my windows as it was going up the Seine, on the 8th day of last May! I thought it looked so pretty, so white and bright! That Being was on board of her, coming from there, where its race originated. And it saw me! It saw my house which was also white, and it sprang from the ship on to the land. Oh, merciful heaven!

Now I know, I can divine. The reign of man is over, and he has come. He who was feared by primitive man; whom disquieted priests exorcised; whom sorcerers evoked on dark nights, without having seen him appear, to whom the imagination of the transient masters of the world lent all the monstrous or graceful forms of gnomes, spirits, genii, fairies and familiar spirits. After the coarse conceptions of primitive fear, more clear-sighted men foresaw it more clearly. Mesmer divined it, and ten years ago physicians accurately discovered the nature of his power, even before he exercised it himself. They played with this new weapon of the Lord, the sway of a mysterious will over the human soul, which had become a slave. They called it magnetism, hypnotism, suggestion—what do I know? I have seen them amusing themselves like rash children with this horrible power! Woe to us! Woe to man! He has come, the—the—what does he call himself—the—I fancy that he is shouting out his name to me and I do not hear him—the—yes—he is shouting it out—I am listening—I cannot— he repeats it—the—Horla—I hear—the Horla—it is he—the Horla— he has come!

Ah! the vulture has eaten the pigeon; the wolf has eaten the lamb; the lion has devoured the sharp-horned buffalo; man has killed the lion with an arrow, with a sword, with gunpowder; but the Horla will make of man what we have made of the horse and of the ox; his chattel, his slave and his food, by the mere power of his will. Woe to us!

But, nevertheless, the animal sometimes revolts and kills the man who has subjugated it. I should also like—I shall be able to—but I must know him, touch him, see him! Scientists say that animals' eyes, being different from ours, do not distinguish objects as ours do. And my eye cannot distinguish this newcomer who is oppressing me.

Why? Oh, now I remember the words of the monk at Mont Saint-Michel: "Can we see the hundred-thousandth part of what exists? See here; there is the wind, which is the strongest force in nature, which knocks down men, and blows down buildings, uproots trees, raises the sea into mountains of water, destroys cliffs and casts great ships on the breakers; the wind which kills, which whistles, which sighs, which roars—have you ever seen it, and can you see it? It exists for all that, however!"

And I went on thinking; my eyes are so weak, so imperfect, that they do not even distinguish hard bodies, if they are as transparent as glass! If a glass without tinfoil behind it were to bar my way, I should run into it, just as a bird which has flown into a room breaks its head against the window-panes. A thousand things, moreover, deceive man and lead him astray. Why should it then be surprising that he cannot perceive an unknown body through which the light passes?

A new being! Why not? It was assuredly bound to come! Why should we be the last? We do not distinguish it any more than all the others created before us! The reason is, that its nature is more perfect, its body finer and more finished than ours, that ours is so weak, so awkwardly constructed, encumbered with organs that are always tired, always on the strain like machinery that is too complicated, which lives like a plant and like a beast, nourishing itself with difficulty on air, herbs and flesh, an animal machine which is a prey to maladies, to malformations, to decay; broken-winded, badly regulated, simple and eccentric, ingeniously badly made, at once a coarse and a delicate piece of workmanship, the rough sketch of a being that might become intelligent and grand.

We are only a few, so few in this world, from the oyster up to man. Why should there not be one more, once that period is passed which separates the successive apparitions from all the different species?

Why not one more? Why not, also, other trees with immense, splendid flowers, perfuming whole regions? Why not other elements besides fire, air, earth and water? There are four, only four, those nursing fathers of various beings! What a pity! Why are there not forty, four hundred, four thousand? How poor everything is, how mean and wretched! grudgingly produced, roughly constructed, clumsily made! Ah, the elephant and the hippopotamus, what grace! And the camel, what elegance!

But the butterfly, you will say, a flying flower! I dream of one that should be as large as a hundred worlds, with wings whose shape, beauty, colors and motion I cannot even express. But I see it—it flutters from star to star, refreshing them and perfuming them with the light and harmonious breath of its flight! And the people up there look at it as it passes in an ecstasy of delight!

*　　　*　　　*

What is the matter with me? It is he, the Horla, who haunts me, and who makes me think of these foolish things! He is within me, he is becoming my soul; I shall kill him!

August 19. I shall kill him. I have seen him! Yesterday I sat down at my table and pretended to write very assiduously. I knew quite well that he would come prowling round me, quite close to me, so close that I might perhaps be able to touch him, to seize him. And then—then I should have the strength of desperation; I should have my hands, my knees, my chest, my forehead, my teeth to strangle him, to crush him, to bite him, to tear him to pieces. And I watched for him with all my over-excited senses.

I had lighted my two lamps and the eight wax candles on my mantelpiece, as if with this light I could discover him.

My bedstead, my old oak post bedstead, stood opposite to me; on my right was the fireplace; on my left, the door which was carefully closed, after I had left it open for some time in order to attract him; behind me was a very high wardrobe with a looking-glass in it, before which I stood to shave and dress every day, and in which I was in the habit of glancing at myself from head to foot every time I passed it.

I pretended to be writing in order to deceive him, for he also was watching me, and suddenly I felt—I was certain that he was reading over my shoulder, that he was there, touching my ear.

I got up, my hands extended, and turned round so quickly that I almost fell. Eh! well? It was as bright as at midday, but I did not see my reflection in the mirror! It was empty, clear, profound, full of light! But my figure was not reflected in it—and I, I was opposite to it! I saw the large, clear glass from top to bottom, and I looked at it with unsteady eyes; and I did not dare to advance; I did not venture to make a movement, feeling that he was there, but that he would escape me again, he whose imperceptible body had absorbed my reflection.

How frightened I was! And then, suddenly, I began to see myself in a mist in the depths of the looking-glass, in a mist as it were a sheet of water; and it seemed to me as if this water were flowing clearer every moment. It was like the end of an eclipse. Whatever it was that hid me did not appear to possess any clearly defined outlines, but a sort of opaque transparency which gradually grew clearer.

At last I was able to distinguish myself completely, as I do every day when I look at myself.

I had seen it! And the horror of it remained with me, and makes me shudder even now.

August 20. How could I kill it, as I could not get hold of it? Poison? But it would see me mix it with the water; and then, would our poisons have any effect on its impalpable body? No—no—no doubt about the matter——Then—then?—

August 21. I sent for a blacksmith from Rouen, and ordered iron shutters for my room, such as some private hotels in Paris have on the ground floor, for fear of burglars, and he is going to make me an iron door as well. I have made myself out a coward, but I do not care about that!

*   *   *

September 10.—Rouen, Hotel Continental. It is done—it is done—but is he dead? My mind is thoroughly upset by what I have seen.

Well then, yesterday, the locksmith having put on the iron shutters and door, I left everything open until midnight, although it was getting cold.

Suddenly I felt that he was there, and joy, mad joy, took possession of me. I got up softly, and walked up and down for some time, so that he might not suspect anything; then I took off my boots and put on my slippers carelessly; then I fastened the iron shutters, and, going back to the door, quickly double-locked it with a padlock, putting the key into my pocket.

Suddenly I noticed that he was moving restlessly round me, that in his turn he was frightened and was ordering me to let him out. I nearly yielded; I did not, however, but, putting my back to the door, I half opened it, just enough to allow me to go out backward, and as I am very tall my head touched the casing. I was sure that he had not been able to escape, and I shut him up quite alone, quite alone. What happiness! I had him fast. Then I ran downstairs; in the drawing-room, which was under my bedroom, I took the two lamps and I poured all the oil on the carpet, the furniture, everywhere; then I set fire to it and made my escape, after having carefully double-locked the door.

I went and hid myself at the bottom of the garden, in a clump of laurel bushes. How long it seemed! How long it seemed! Everything was dark, silent, motionless, not a breath of air and not a star, but heavy banks of clouds which one could not see, but which weighed, oh, so heavily on my soul.

I looked at my house and waited. How long it was! I already began to think that the fire had gone out of its own accord, or that he had extinguished it, when one of the lower windows gave way under the violence of the flames, and a long, soft, caressing sheet of red flame mounted up the white wall, and enveloped it as far as the roof. The light fell on the trees, the branches, and the leaves, and a shiver of fear pervaded them also! The birds awoke, a dog began to howl, and it seemed to me as if the day were breaking! Almost immediately two other windows flew into fragments, and I saw that the whole of the lower part of my house was nothing but a terrible furnace. But a cry, a horrible, shrill, heartrending cry, a woman's cry, sounded through the night, and two garret windows were opened! I had forgotten the servants! I saw their terror-stricken faces, and their arms waving frantically.

Then, overwhelmed with horror, I set off to run to the village, shouting: "Help! help! fire! fire!" I met some people who were already coming to the scene, and I returned with them.

By this time the house was nothing but a horrible and magnificent funeral pile, a monstrous funeral pile which lit up the whole country, a funeral pile where men were burning, and where he was burning also, He, He, my prisoner, that new Being, the new master, the Horla!

Suddenly the whole roof fell in between the walls, and a volcano of flames darted up to the sky. Through all the windows which opened on that furnace, I saw the flames darting, and I thought that he was there, in that kiln, dead.

Dead? Perhaps?——His body? Was not his body, which was transparent, indestructible by such means as would kill ours?

If he were not dead?——Perhaps time alone has power over that Invisible and Redoubtable Being. Why this transparent, unrecognizable body, this body belonging to a spirit, if it also has to fear ills, infirmities and premature destruction?

Premature destruction? All human terror springs from that! After man, the Horla. After him who can die every day, at any hour, at any moment, by any accident, came the one who would die only at his own proper hour, day, and minute, because he had touched the limits of his existence!

No—no—without any doubt—he is not dead——Then—then—I suppose I must kill myself! . . .